2020

After the End

Bill de Garis

This edition published 2016

ISBN: 0993681700

ISBN-13: 978-0993681707

For Doreen and Willy.

Front cover scene: The Cabin.

Back cover scene: The beach at Baja.

This is book 1 of the 2020 series
Book 2: **2020 The Long Walk**
Book 3: **2020 Africa**

Contents

I couldn't have published this without my good friend Christy Williams Richards editing and correcting all my mistakes and making many great suggestions. Thanks also to Keith Roper, Heather Wall, Bob Kent, Granville Davies and Darryl Ware.

Chapter 1, What the hell is going on?

We live pretty much all our lives inside now.

It is the year 2020 and we live pretty much all our lives inside now. It is either too hot or too cold outside in the Wild. Autumn and spring are nice, so that is when we repair our buildings. We have heat dishes that track the sun and we store the heat underground for the long winter when there is no warmth from the sun. We grow all the food we need in our domes and there are plenty of recreation rooms where, with our friends, we can lose a few pounds around our waist, or a few hours surrounded in audio and video fantasy.

We have a good life inside... but I'm getting ahead of myself. This story begins many thousands of years ago in the old years of the early humans, back in the beginning of what they called the "new millennium" in the 21st century. Back when our ancestors ruled the world and even thought they could rule the solar system and perhaps even the universe some day.

Oh, we used to have a few problems now and then: a disease would spread amongst us or the wind and rain would take over, temporarily. Or an earthquake or volcano would slow us down, but not for long; no matter how many of us died it hardly slowed us down at all. We kept multiplying. It was what we did best.

But one day a special virus hit us, one that was implanted in our genes. A virus so close to home that we never had a chance; we never saw it coming.

That virus was us.

It was just after the turn of the millennium, and autumn in British Columbia, on the coast of the Pacific Northwest of North America. Autumn was a truly magical time of year there. The clouds were clinging to the tops of the hillsides around where "the gang" were riding their Trials motorcycles in the forest. They were at a place they called "The Holiday Camp". It was called that because riding Trials there was anything but a holiday!

A 'Hulking Great Rock'

Right next to them the inlet led through the harbour and eventually all the way to the Pacific Ocean. The air was fresh and clean and crisp after several days of rain, and the sun was shafting through the trees. This time of year it was never more than pleasantly warm even in the afternoon. A helicopter hidden overhead by the trees beat its way down the inlet, its thumping urgent sound very violent and foreign in the lush green stillness. The helicopter quickly faded away to nothing. Peter (PJ as everyone called him) looked up but saw nothing and was reminded by the sound of that horrific brilliant movie Apocalypse

Now.

He looked at the gang scattered around him some sitting on their motorbikes resting, while the others were practising Trials. The young twenty-something boys were challenging each other on a huge vertical rock face, fighting to be the first to ride up the hulking great rock “clean” (without using their feet), while the yet teen-aged girls sat on their bikes and smiled at each other. They knew what the young men were really doing.

Being there to catch the bike...

The fathers were looking out for their rapidly growing up kids: being there to catch the bike when the kids failed and tumbled back off the rocks and big walls. They still did this for their kids even though they didn’t have to pay for the motorbike repairs any more. The fathers were still part of the team and still living their own dreams vicariously through their kids.

The girls were fun to ride with for those without kids and well past their prime. They didn’t do the crazy big obstacles the boys were trying but they were getting there. It was lovely days like this that PJ thought sadly about what they would all do when the girls left to start families of their own. It would happen so quickly, before they knew it. Then the fun times would be gone, leaving just one or two other old men for him to ride with on easy obstacles that would not break their bodies if they crashed off them. Wheelchair riding was what PJ called it and he wasn't ready for it yet. The girls might come back and ride again but by that time in their lives they would have kids in tow on mini bikes. Anyway by then he would be long gone. It was a good time to be in this part of the world. The sounds of war had not reached them from the far off countries where they were sending their young men out to fight and die in. Yes, this was still a quiet and peaceful place to be. They didn't know it but those far off sounds of war were coming closer faster, far faster than they could ever live their lives.

The years that followed were pretty ordinary times in BC. Kids grew up and got married, and had kids. Families moved in search of a better life or job. People got angry or scared or fell in love. People fell ill and got better, or died. Babies took their place. Outrageous things happened, or didn't happen. People fought the ravages of time on their body as they had always done... with exercise or patent remedies or just plain hope. But as ever they slipped quietly into old age or were dragged there kicking and screaming. Once there they never returned, and their senses drifted away while their world became a quieter and more peaceful place to be. The young had limitless dreams to look forward to, the middle aged limitless debt, while the old just had their old dreams and limitless death. It seemed completely unlikely that anything overwhelmingly disastrous would happen, why should it? The chances were that life would go on just as normal in their increasingly safe and always modern world. A world obsessed with painting white lines which they must not cross and insisting they wear safety helmets while walking in the forest... if they were within the white lines that is. A world so taken up with meaningless dialogue and rules that workers in a park, sweeping a path in the forest glades to free it of leaves, were required to wear head-to-toe bright orange clothing with reflective stripes and steel-toed boots. Dangerous stuff, leaves. Perhaps they were worried that small rodents in the trees or maybe birds might run into them, or mistake them for something that was good to eat.

But regardless of our follies and sweeping, the leaves kept falling. Then one day, one truly awful day—out of the darkness of space and completely unannounced, came a huge meteorite. Its passage through the atmosphere lit up the night sky all around the globe and its sound and shock waves were felt for thousands of miles as it smashed into the mountains somewhere north of India. It was like the earth was tearing apart at its very core. Huge ocean waves wiped clean most of the low-lying lands around the world, and with it most of the life; in particular human life because the low lands were where most of us preferred to live. And then there were devastating earthquakes and volcanic eruptions along the fault lines all over the world, triggered by the meteorite.

But the chunk of rock that hit the earth was only a fragmented part of a much bigger meteor that just missed. That one was huge and had a mass about half that of our moon. Almost no one saw this monster because of all the dust and smoke and chaos going on, but it had a truly devastating effect. The gravitational tug from the meteor altered the earth's axis, and even her orbit around the sun was changed. The meteor sped off, heading back into deep space hopefully never to return, leaving behind an earth seemingly crippled and beyond all hope. In this awful time the people that were left alive began to realise that for all those years the doom sayers had been wrong, they finally got it right... the end of the world had come. But what no one knew yet was that with the change in the axis and tilt of the earth the year had changed, lengthened to two and a half times what it was before. This was going to have the most devastating long term effect of all.

We might have recovered soon enough if this had been all that had occurred. If we'd had a chance to realise that the earth was slower and the year was longer... hah! No such luck... A group of fanatics in some far off country saw this as a sign that their time had come to redress the old wrongs and advance the cause of their beliefs. Within a few hours of the meteor strike they took over the nuclear weapons in the silos of Pakistan and attempted to release them at India. They were quite successful, most went there but some were targeted at China and other countries and some may have just gone rogue. Who knows? They were fanatics, not nuclear physicists. All they knew was, BOOM.

China and India retaliated, and then North Korea saw its chance and sent off two missiles at cities on the west coast of the US and short range missiles to South Korea and Japan. It was mayhem. Israel was targeted by Iran and retaliated with massive force against all of its numerous enemies. With both the Middle and Far East in flames and a few of their own cities too, Russia and the US joined in even though they couldn't be sure where some of the missiles had come from. Citizens in both countries were demanding retaliation (though most called it justice). Finally, every country in the world with nuclear weapons was drawn into releasing their arsenal as one or another of their cities was obliterated. There was a point in time when it became impossible to tell whose missiles were wiping out which cities since there were so many warheads in the sky all at once.

In addition to the nukes creating their huge, instant death and destruction, and their legacy of a half-life of thousands of years of deadly radiation, there was yet another massive blow to our infrastructure. One of the things the military had done without telling anyone was to create a class of killer satellites that targeted their enemies' satellites and not just the military ones... the civilian communication and navigation satellites as well. So following the missiles came a rain of satellite debris streaking across the sky and slamming into the earth. It all happened so very quickly, hours, not days, and for most of us far too quickly for rational thought to take hold. Just, *boom* and it had started and finished.

It was a perfectly ordinary Friday towards the end of summer. A bit hot in the streets of Seattle but real pleasant inside the coffee shop. Kate finished off her latte and walked outside. As the hot blast of air outside hit her, *boom*, there was a blinding flash of light that lasted for a fraction of a second in her mind. Dave was rushing through the down-town traffic. He was late getting back from lunch but he had a great lead on a set of condo's coming on the market. The lights turned red before he could get through them, then *boom* everything turned white for the instant in time that was all the time he had left. Now there were no Kate or Dave, nothing, actually; just silence in the space where their minds had once been. But it was not the sort of silence you and I can imagine. It was the silence of Hell.

PJ had the front door open at his house in Port Moody, British Columbia, still letting in the fresh outside air although it was no longer cool. He had to mow the lawn today sometime. He was sitting at the computer and dreaming while he typed. The computer gave him a friendly belch "Bollocks—Oh dear me!" It was his signature belch and it meant an email had arrived. He read and deleted it, someone was trying to sell him some software he didn't need, then he paused, what was he thinking about? Oh yes, how to get the main characters into trouble, he needed more excitement in the story. Guess it could be anywhere. How about... *boom*.

He lifted his head and listened. That came from a long way away. Strange, it was a bit like the day he had heard Mount St Helens blow her top, back in, what was it, 1980? He had heard it while he was lying in bed in his caravan at a trailer park near Port Moody having a bit of a sleep in. A boom rather like this one but more distant. Fancy hearing an explosion that was several hundred miles away. Mount St Helens was big though. This one sounded closer but it was still big and it had an ominous rumbling with it. Maybe something had gone wrong with one of the refineries. Then his backup power supply kicked in as the power went off. Beep beep beep... He shut down his computer and prepared to wait out the beeping until the UPS lost its charge. Then he could enjoy the neighbourhood in silence. Damn, this shut-down was the perfect time to mow the lawn; except his lawnmower was electric. "Oh well, may as well get out the camp stove and make a cup of tea," he said to himself.

Mike and Kacie were listening to the news on their pickups radio when the signal went away like it had been chopped by an axe. They tried a few more stations but all they got was static and some tiny outfit inland pumping out country music.

"Power cut?" suggested Mike.

"Seems a bit strange," said Kacie, "all of them going off like that. Don't they have backup power?" They turned the radio off and the cab went completely silent. They turned the radio off and the cab went completely silent. They were only sixty miles from their summer cabin up north, up near the headwaters of the Yalakom river in central British Columbia.

Jeff was chopping wood at the cabin when they arrived "There's something big going on. I was picking up groceries in the village when one of those emergency messages came over the local station. I stocked up on food just in case. I think we better plan on spending more than just the long weekend up here."

"Yeah, well the radio went blank on us so we shut it off," said Mike.

"We thought it was just a major power cut," said Kacie. "I wonder if some jerk-off government finally did something really stupid?"

It was the beginning of the future, perhaps the year after next year. But definitely not the year anyone ever wanted to see. They listened to the news on shortwave and got gossip and rumour from the village. As near as the three of them could make out everyone had just got madder than all get-out and in a tit-for-tat escalation started throwing everything they had at everyone else. It was just like the days when we were barely more than apes, only this time we were chucking nukes instead of stones and the awful shock-waves and nuclear winds ripped apart just about every major city in the world. That, and the smoke and dust in the sky from the meteor really screwed things up. It was as if life had slowed down to a crawl, which it pretty much had. In a very short while there was no structure any more, no government and no order, except for that which small bands of people made. How many thousands of years had it taken to create civilisation? It took only a few days to destroy.

Initially in those places that weren't hit by the nukes, like Vancouver, there had been mayhem; huge fires and mass riots and killings when the food ran out. The electromagnetic waves from the nukes wiped out just about every microprocessor in the developed world. Most of the "smart" devices we used everyday just stopped working. No more smart phones or smart cars. In a very short while there was no electricity or heating gas and no oil or gasoline of course, and eventually no water. Almost nothing moved except on foot, and the roads were littered with vehicles, bodies, fallen trees and accumulating rubbish. People got together in convoys with hired guards to help them get out of the city, to somewhere where they thought they might be able to survive—like the Okanagen, but the Okanagen didn't want any more people. These convoys were turned away and became death marches... Marches where you got so tired and hungry you could barely move one leg in front of the other and your eyes blurred so you could not recognize anyone and there was just a ringing and heart throbbing pounding in your ears. Then you were happy to lie down on the side of the road and die.

For month after month dust and smoke circled the

globe—creating an eerie swirling fog of dirt grey clouds mixed with strange lights streaking across the upper atmosphere. But the eeriest thing of all was the silence, everything was so quiet. No planes filled the sky with the roar of their engines; there were no trains rumbling along their tracks with their huge diesel engines beating in and out of sync like the sound track in a B grade horror movie, gone also were the trains' air horns that blasted your mind and left your ears ringing. The construction jack-hammers were silent, the tower cranes motionless on top of the huge office buildings. These buildings now just barren dying skeletons of grey concrete streaked black by water—overlooking empty yards where trucks and people had once been. And the roar of traffic had completely gone. It was like the morning of Christmas day when everyone is still at home opening their presents and all the world outside is silent. When the dust clouds finally went away, the sound of the city was the eerie quiet of a forest of silent buildings; roads littered with broken glass and debris from crumbling structures, and draped over them—hanging wires with loose panels flapping in the breeze. There was no one walking on the streets. If you had to go outside, you ran. It was like a scene from some famous directors movie of one of the Balkan wars. Only this time it was for real.

Then there was the night time; ahh yes, the night time when only animals moved and hunted, and for the first time in so many lifetimes a man could stand in the darkness in the innermost centre of the city, look up at the night sky, and see the Milky Way like the sprinkling of a million glow-worms on the roof of the huge black cave of the universe.

What about the police and the military and the civil defence? What happened to the disaster relief plans and the aid organisations? Well, basically, they're just a proxy for us. We're supposed to help them. What about your neighbours, your friends, your family? It doesn't work. What good is it when it's all gone, and all the people who are supposed to help you can't even help themselves?

Everything was looted and those people that survived did so with what little they had hoarded. There were no such things as work and play any more, only life and death; and there was plenty of death. The fires were apocalyptic. Throughout the world huge forests burned unchecked in the heat of that first extended summer. Smoke travelled the roof of the world and until the first hint of autumn there was only night and half-night, day after day. Country folks had some chance in the short term, but the urban people? None at all. How does someone survive whose life skills are being able to drive a temperature controlled SUV to a climate controlled supermarket to buy a bunch of dead things sprayed with lethal radiation so they lasted long enough for them to eat? If the micro-organisms wouldn't eat this stuff how come the people were not so smart? At home the touch of a button provided dinner, and the touch of another button entertainment. How could these pampered and molly-coddled people survive...

in the raw...

outside...

on foot...

in an urban desert that has no rules?

It was amazing how quickly it all fell apart.

Chapter 2, The Cabin.

The cabin

In Port Moody, PJ stayed at home and kept to himself. He lived in a quiet suburb where the only sounds had been the neighbours dogs, the float planes droning off into the interior, and the subdued traffic noise and trains from across the other side of the inlet. There were awful things happening if you went out looking for food or help so he stayed at home. He got out the Coleman lantern and the old Coleman kerosene stove; dug out the emergency candles and found enough batteries to listen every now and then to the shortwave. He filled the bathtub up with water and all his camping water containers, too. Who knew how long the water supply would last? PJ was 45 years old, five foot six inches tall, and quite fit. He wrote short stories for magazines to supplement a small investment income, and when he wasn't writing (which was often) you would find him in his garden growing his own food or out playing on his Trials motorbike in the forest. He normally lived alone so no one bothered him. To make sure, he kept his blinds down and listened occasionally from his upstairs bedroom window to the sounds of the city slowly dying away. There were no sounds from his house; without electricity he couldn't play music or watch films or make any noise at all and he tried not to let the lantern be visible from the outside at night.

Normally he had no problems living alone, it was peaceful, and there were no hassles. But it was, ahh, a little freaky now without TV or the internet. And there was no option to email his friends and say: "What's up guys. Wanna go riding this morning?" When your whole life has been immersed in sound on demand, enforced silence is pretty unnerving. Boring too. None of his toys worked; the camera, the sound recorder, the personal computer. Whoa, dude this was not good! He wised up fast when things started to go real quiet; after a few days there was no more traffic noise and he heard the silence coming across the waters of the inlet. His neighbours didn't go out driving now. Occasionally he would see them standing together in the road. They looked nervous and most of them were scared. The radio was full of awful things happening apparently everywhere, but there was not a lot of local news. Then the water ran out. He watched it trickling slowly at first into the kitchen sink and then so quickly, nothing. Well that was it. You couldn't live without water. Seriously, you could last weeks without food, but water?

Fortunately he had filled up his pickup a few days before "The Big Bang" as he called it. He had gotten a bunch of food at the supermarket at the same time. Just as well, you wouldn't be able to buy food or gas now: they close the tills when the power fails and shut the doors. Everything shuts down when the power fails.

He began loading his pickup with his Trials bike and survival gear, mostly just his normal camping gear: tent, backpack, poncho, etc, and his old hiking stuff that he hadn't used since he permanently damaged his ankle, oh, 20 years ago now. The hiking boots were still best for walking in, bad ankle or not, and they would do good enough on the bike if he had to ride. Then he began packing up everything he thought he could use on the road. It was just like going to a Trials competition so he was well used to it. He had started as usual by loading his Gas Gas Trials bike and the bulky stuff like his pack, gas-cans and toolbox. Now he was filling in all the nooks and crannies with spare shoes and boots and individual items of clothing. Early the next morning before dawn he went out to his garden but left the slugs alone this time crawling along after their evening meal. He picked a bunch of salad greens and all the ripe and near ripe tomatoes and sweetcorn. Then he looked around at the rest of the garden still growing for an uncertain future. "The slugs will have a field day now," he said to himself, "Oh well..." Then he had a bite to eat and a cup of coffee and carried on packing stuff into his pickup, occasionally pulling stuff out and replacing it with something more important.

The biggest difference between this and a competition was this was probably going to be for a very long time, not just a few weeks, so he had to think of things that he couldn't do without. But he needed all his stuff, otherwise he wouldn't have it. Right? So he loaded up his pickup until it was almost full, shoved his sleeping gear on top, and left the rest. Hey, you never know, he might come back one day. It was late afternoon when he had finished so he took one final look around the house making sure the windows were closed and all the circuit breakers were off and that there was nothing sitting anywhere that he absolutely had to have with him. Then he sighed and locked the door of his house. He sat down in the drivers seat of his pickup, closed the door and looked around him at all the stuff piled everywhere in every available space. Then he glanced through the rear window at his Gas Gas and the mountain of stuff under the canopy in the back. He remembered not to buckle up his seatbelt; he wanted to be able to get out quickly and either run or defend himself if necessary. He just sat there for awhile and stared out through the windshield. It was a blank page, now, his life. What was going to happen? He took a deep breath and fired up the engine, got first gear and drove very slowly and carefully away from his home, forever.

It was dusk as he set off up the Lougheed highway, heading east towards Hope. It was weird passing through the darkening and silent streets in Maple Ridge where once there had been permanent light, day or night. Now when the night came both the forest *and* the city turned dark. It was dark enough that he saw no one and he drove quickly up through Mission, past Hope onto Highway 1, and headed up the Fraser Valley. Where was he going? He shrugged his shoulders, sighed and answered the same as every traveller heading for a new life on the open road: "Who knows?" Then he thought: what about his riding buddies, Kacie, Mike, and Jeff. Didn't they have a cabin up this way? Where was it again? Damn, he couldn't remember.

The days were real long now and it felt like the middle of summer. Miserably hot, too. But we had already had the middle of summer, months ago. He parked off in a copse of trees on a side road and slept in the back of his pickup rather uncomfortably on top of the jumble of stuff there. The next day he was up near Spuzzum when he remembered where his friends were... the other side of Lillooet way up high in the surrounding hills and mountains. Up by the headwaters of the Yalakom river. But *exactly* where? Oh hell, he wasn't going anywhere special, may as well just drive up that way and ask.

Lillooet has the unenviable reputation as the hottest place in BC in the summer and it didn't disappoint, it was like being in an oven and there didn't seem to be anybody around. But eventually he found someone who directed him to someone else who might be able to help. "Take Moha road east out of town," the second person said. "This turns into Bridge River road just after you cross the Yalakom river. About 15 K later turn right onto Yalakom road and follow it north. About 40 minutes later, depending on how fast you're travelling, you'll take a road on your right going up a hill. I'm not sure how much further on but you take a track on the right. Leads straight to your friends place."

At the cabin Kacie had come back from the stream with water and was heating some in a kettle, waiting for Mike and Jeff to return from the forest—when PJ drove up with a big stupid grin on his face! Kacie owned a couple of flower shops and kept fit jogging and conducting exercise classes. She was 25, five foot ten, slim and very fit. She talked in that fast, almost frantic way that young people did nowadays. A stream of words so close together they were mostly unintelligible to PJ. Each stream was followed by a short pause and then came the next rapid blast of word-like sounds. It was as though the ideas behind the words were so fragile; if they were not expressed immediately they would be lost. But when said slowly perhaps their true lack of meaning would be known, even to her. Her husband Mike was 35; he owned an electrical contracting firm. He was six feet tall and liked to play golf. He wasn't very fit but at his age, who cares? Jeff was 65, retired, and an all-around nice guy who never said a bad word to anyone (although PJ managed to bring out a tougher streak in him now and then). Jeff was a little under six feet and had been super fit when he was younger, but he was still very much in shape for his age.

Mike had shot a deer and he and Jeff had partially butchered the carcass and strapped it to their packs. They would have to smoke and dry it tomorrow. All three of them were super pleased to see PJ. He was a good gardener and they all knew food was the number one priority.

"Man it's so nice to be among friends," said PJ. "You get real hyper living alone in times like these. Things that go bump in the night; know what I mean?"

Kacie smiled. "I know what you mean."

"I can imagine it must be pretty lonely hanging out on your own in these times," said Jeff. "You were lucky to hook up with us from the sound of things."

"Hell I couldn't have lasted long at my house," said PJ, "No water, only vegetables. Geez. I don't like the thought of trying to live in the Lower Mainland, I mean even if you have your own vegetable garden you're not going to make it more than once through the winter, not with our low level of expertise at hunting. And while your out hunting everyone else is going to be poaching from your garden. What are you going to do—stay at home and die saving your tomatoes?"

"You were a vegetarian at one time," said Kacie, "why not again?"

"Yeah, I lasted a couple of months and then got so weak I could hardly ride my Gasser!"

"This is the best place we could be," said Jeff, "There's a ton of game all round us. We'll be just fine—as long as we don't want to be vegetarians!"

"Yes, we're not going to be growing anything up this high in winter," said PJ.

"We're safe here right now," added Mike. "But what are we going to do long term?"

Kacie leaned forwards and kissed him "One day at a time."

The four of them stayed at the cabin as the news trickled through to them on shortwave. Things appeared to be collapsing fast. A month went by and the snippets of news from the village were not good. Apparently Vancouver was impossible to travel through with roadblocks guarded by gangs that would as soon murder you as let you pass, even if you could pay the toll. Money of course was no good any more. Food, fuel, and weapons were the trading currencies now. And weapons came out on top every time. Their summer cabin in central British Columbia was turning out to be a good place to live in these bad times; up country and away from the murder and death that had been the end so far of all the expectations of the world.

They didn't bother going down to the village now, there was nothing left on the shelves and very few people around. Most everyone had moved off to join relatives elsewhere. People in the village didn't talk much any more, it was like a chill had taken over their lives. If you saw someone, their eyes were hooded and they ducked away back into the shadows before you could approach them.

It was now three months into autumn and getting colder. Autumn was already three months? Summer of course had been almost unbearably hot even as high up as they were, but now it was starting to get cold. It was weird, summer had seemed to last forever; almost like it was a whole year long.

PJ looked around at the autumn leaves "This is the middle of January now, the middle of winter, and we're just coming to the end of autumn. What the hell is going on?"

They had everything they needed at the cabin; hunting bows and knives, packs and camping gear, winter clothes and provisions—they even had their trail bikes with the big gas tanks so they could go for expeditions up into the mountains. PJ had his Gas Gas Trials bike in the back of his pickup, it had a tiny gas tank and no seat of course (Trials bikes are ridden standing up), but it was a motorbike and that sucker could go almost anywhere off road. All three of their pickup trucks were parked for good now, the access road had downed trees that made it impassible except with the trail bikes.

In the early afternoon it was warm enough to be very pleasant so they sat around outside under the trees, sheltered from the cool light wind while lunch settled down. A birds nest lay on the ground under one of the trees, the carefully woven grass dry and empty. Beside it in the midst of the moss and weeds and the twigs fallen from the tree were the paper-thin remains of two eggs cracked and broken apart. Still bright blue-green but now just empty shells without any trace that they were once full of life. Did the hatchlings make it? Or had some predator got to the nest first and scored a juicy meal?

"How come you never married PJ?" asked Kacie.

"Oh I was thinking I would once upon a time, long ago. There was this neat gal I was dating. We were lying back in bed one afternoon on the weekend and she said something about getting a double bed. I said I would never get used to sleeping with another person in the same bed. It takes me sometimes hours of tossing and turning from side to side, putting my feet over the end of the bed this way and that, and sometimes draping an arm over the side, before the magic happens and I wake up and it's morning. I said we would have to have separate beds and probably separate rooms. She was not amused and split not long after that."

"You let her walk away."

"Yes, I figured she wouldn't have any trouble finding a good husband, she was one of those gal's who really had no bad side, except she liked country music, and I can't stand listening to that!"

"She liked country music so you let her walk away... Honestly PJ you really are dumb sometimes!"

A bird perched on top of the top-most part of a young fir tree, bending the thin stem horizontal and curving the top down towards the ground as though it had wilted long ago in the middle of summer's long drought. It was well past midday, the sun was low and almost halfway across the southern sky. The day had that lazier more slowly moving air about it now. There was a scent of grass drying, and in the almost still air the smell of... nothing at all going on. The sun had some warmth, but not enough to keep you warm if you stood still. The past few days had been a little weird; the deer had been migrating through their valley. They had never come this way before in such numbers. At night in the mist it was like watching an army of ghosts drifting silently and slowly through the trees. Occasionally an animal would raise its head, pause and look at them, then turn away and disappear back into the whiteness. It was almost as though the deer were trying to tell them something. That evening at the cabin they talked about the future over a cup of tea.

They would have to get used to life without tea.

“We’re going to have to learn how to make ‘erbal tea,” said Jeff.

“Unggh!” said PJ. “I don’t really like herbal tea. I drink Ceylon tea, with milk of course. Mind you I like a nice cup-a-Joe to start the morning off.”

“It’s going to have to be ‘erbal tea, PJ,” stated Kacie. “Nothing else grows in these parts. You’re the gardener, you know that.”

PJ gritted his teeth, made a face and grinned ruefully. “Bummer, you’re right of course. Guess I’ll live with it. Gonna be a shake-up though, and not just for my taste buds. Herbal tea. Yikes!”

With only the firelight inside the cabin they stared at the flames and their eyes were alive with the soft red and black flickering shadows around them. The fire crackled and snuffled away quietly to itself and there was silence for awhile.

It was Kacie who said it first... “We’re probably not going to live through the winter.” Jeff and PJ were looking at the glowing embers in the fire, Mike and Kacie were looking at the reflections of the fire in each others eyes.

PJ looked up “The deer know. We have to go south, on the bikes. Get as far as we can with all the gas we can carry, and then walk.”

Mike looked nervous. “To Mexico?”

“Just as far as we have to go to get away from the cold. Summer was over ten months. Winter will be like an ice age. No one who stays here will live. What are we going to do for food? Look, we know we’re heading into a very long winter. We’ll almost certainly be snowed in. There may not be any game to hunt and we can't grow anything, not in a log cabin thousands of feet up on the edge of the forest in the middle of nowhere, in winter. We're screwed. We want to live? We gotta move south." PJ paused. "We can't take the pickups, we'll never get through, the roads are too bad. We can do it on the bikes though. They'll get us past the radiation at Seattle if we keep to the foothills of the Cascades. We can either go up Highway 2 all the way to Wenatchee or cut across to North Bend at Monroe and make it over Snoqualmie Pass."

"The road to North Bend might be too close to the radiation," suggested Jeff.

"Well, we can make up our minds when we get there," PJ had a cheap military surplus radiation meter.

Mike still had his doubts. "We'll have to be real careful to keep away from," he paused, "trouble."

Everyone knew what trouble meant. Militias in the US with frightening arrays of weapons and enough ammunition to last their lifetime, and several other people's lifetimes as well.

"What are we going to do about my Gasser?" asked PJ. "It's got no range at all. Maybe 50 miles if you're lucky."

"We've got to use our bikes; there's no other way to get through," said Jeff. "We can put some racks on either side of the engine, extend the frame back, and hang stuff there on our trail bikes. But it's going to be difficult with your bike because the frame is so light. Oh I reckon we can cobble something together. Hell, it doesn't have to last, so what if it cracks the frame, this is a one time deal!"

PJ looked thoughtful. "I can use a bit of foam from my pickup to sit on, maybe from the two small jump seats at the back, and carry my pack strapped to my back with my gear in it."

"We're all going to have to carry packs," said Jeff. "Maybe you can hang a few plastic containers of gas from the handlebars. Strap them either side of the headlight. Did you bring the headlight?"

"Yes, I figured it might come in handy."

Mike was still not happy. "How do we know winter will be bad?"

"I know," said Kacie and Jeff nodded. He could feel it in the very core of his being. It was like suddenly growing very old. One day you were 40 and the next when you looked in the mirror you were 65. You knew there wasn't long to go when that feeling came, and he had that feeling now.

They stayed in front of the fire late that night, talking and planning. Kacie was pregnant. They needed to be safe in Mexico before she became too big to travel. It took them almost a week to get sorted, this wasn't a day jaunt or even a big move. They knew that this was quite likely for ever.

It's a strange feeling watching your life change so completely. It's like leaning over the guard rail at the stern of an ocean liner when you leave port, when you're heading for a new country to start your life over again. You watch your whole world fade into the distance. Everything that was so important to you just doesn't matter any more, your old world simply no longer exists. The good thing about ocean journeys in an age before cell phones and jet planes was: they took time, and we humans need time to change. Day after day as you lean over the stern of the ship and look down at the wake, slowly and inexorably every part of what you were is erased for ever. All that's left is the noise of the ships wake, the wind, some seagulls floating like driftwood in the sky, and the throb of the giant engines felt lightly throughout the ship and through every part of your body. Together with the constant movement from the rolling ocean swell, it all means change and freedom from the past. If you go back years or even months later things there have changed without you and it is not your home any more. Now you have a new home.

No wonder sailors love the sea.

Chapter 3, The First Step.

Finally, very early one morning, it was time to leave. They had made the decision the previous afternoon but none of them had been able to sleep. Mike was up making a pot of coffee. With that good smell floating around everyone else snuggled under and wriggled their bodies to get the last bit of stored heat from beneath the covers, and then one by one they all got up, dressed super quick and mooched around sipping coffee.

"If we can't sleep," said Jeff, "what the hell, we may as well get going, eh."

The fire was stoked up for the last time so they could start out warm, then they got the bikes out in front of the cabin and PJ checked the gas tanks one last time to see if they were still full.

PJ looked around at everyone. "We need to be real slow on acceleration and real easy on the brakes. Coast downhill everywhere you can. On the long downhills, get neutral then turn off the engine and free-wheel, huh?"

Everyone nodded their heads; they were all good on bikes and everyone except Mike had competition Trials bikes at home. With their Trials bikes they could ride off-road over the most difficult terrain, the sort of stuff you would have trouble scrambling up using your hands as well as your feet. They had hidden the gas they had left and everything of value for survival underneath the cabin, and then disguised the entrance. You could walk all round the place now and not see it. Who knows if they would be back, but hey, it was there if they ever did return.

They were all going to balance a gallon plastic can full of gas between their knees resting against the bike's gas tank. To hold it steady each can would be strapped to their waists. Instead of the small can, PJ had a larger two and a half gallon one; it was the best he could do to make up for his Gasser's tank being less than a quarter the size of the big tanks on the Yamahas. Together with the other small cans they had cobbled on to his Gas Gas it would give him about the same range as the other bikes. The strap had a quick release so he could ditch the big can real fast in an emergency.

They started the bikes to get them warmed up and then shouldered their packs. Now they rested the small gas cans on the bike's gas tank in front of them and strapped the cans to their waists. Then they climbed carefully on to the bikes. When everyone was ready they couldn't resist taking one last farewell look at the warmth and safety of the cabin. The look lingered but they forced their eyes away, got first gear and rode slowly down the path. There was a whole bunch of wobbling around until they got their natural balance adjusted to the weight and clumsiness of the overladen bikes. They had no time to feel sad or apprehensive what with the excitement of heading into the unknown, plus the difficulty of riding the bikes as heavy as they were... the starter's flag had dropped, now all they had to do was ride as well as they knew how. Where they finished was in the lap of the gods.

They all had extra gas cans strapped on either side of the engine and a gear bag strapped to a small rack behind the rear seat. Except the Gas Gas couldn't have anything strapped behind the foam where the seat should be as there was no rear frame to tie on to, so PJ had to take all of the weight of his pack on his shoulders. For the Yamahas the packs rested on the gear bag at the back and were held upright by the straps over their shoulders and around their waists. Their bows were strapped on the outside of their packs. They figured on getting only two, maybe three days out of the gas they had and then they would be on foot. It depended so much on what the conditions were like, and whether they could scavenge any gas on the trip down. There was no way to know anything about this trip, except they knew that this would be the journey of their lives.

It was quite dark when they left and they travelled like the ghosts of the migrating deer south down through the valleys of the Fraser river. They had made it to just north of Boston Bar when they came across a family in an old Dodge van. The family had escaped from the Maple Ridge area together with some friends.

"There's a roadblock at the bridge by Hope. We got through, our friends didn't," said the husband. "Don't go south, you'll be killed like our friends." His voice choked off.

"The road's closed the other side of Lytton, so we can't get to Merritt and go south from there," said PJ.

"Why are you going south?" asked the husband. "It's bloody murder down in the States. Seattle got nuked and the survivors fought each other to escape. There's no food there, just like the Lower Mainland. It's why we left."

"We think the winter up here will be too cold to live through," said Kacie.

"We've got family up in Lytton on a farm, that's where we're going, we'll be safe there. Come with us. You'll be very welcome." His kids and wife were looking at them from inside the van. They looked scared.

"No. But thanks," said PJ. "We're going way south, probably Mexico."

Mike turned round and looked at everyone. "Oh man, what are we going to do now?"

"There's a back way to Harrison Lake from Boston Bar," said PJ to Mike, then to the husband. "Do you know if any of the bridges across the Fraser are open, south of Hope?"

"We don't know about the bridges but we had some problems getting up the Lougheed to Hope where the roadblock is. There are washouts on the road and we had to winch our way across them. You should get through OK on the bikes. There was a huge tidal wave that came through, made a mess of the place."

"Back way?" said Jeff. "There's no back way to Harrison Lake from here. There's just this road!"

"There's a bunch of logging roads and forestry tracks all around us," explained PJ. "Just north of here on the other side of the river one of them comes out at Harrison Hot Springs. The others dead end. I drove all the way in my pickup once when I was researching a story."

Kacie looked impressed. "All the way to Harrison Hot Springs?"

"Yep. From Boston Bar. There's a few tricky bits for a two wheel drive like my pickup, but nothing a trail bike can't handle even loaded like we are. It's a good way to go if there haven't been any rock slides, but there are a few places where slides are common. The trail follows a bunch of valleys and goes up to about three and a half, maybe four thousand feet, if I remember right." PJ looked around at them all. "There's a bridge at Boston Bar, we can cross there."

The others were not convinced. The hills and mountains around them were on the edge of the wilderness and were the natural home of bears and cougars. A scary place to be if you didn't know your way. Mike broke the silence. "You think there will be snow on the trail, if it's still passable?"

"No way to be sure if there's snow. But I don't think so right now. Biggest unknown is if we can get the bikes through if there are slides. I used to bushwhack in Africa. Bundu bashing we called it. There were times when we had to carry the bikes up escarpments. Well, one time anyway. And those were trail bikes like these Yamahas," he paused. "Oh hell, if there's no slides it'll be a piece a piss. We can portage if we have to, we did that in the Sahara with the old Morris Isis we had, pull everything off and carry it over the bad parts on foot, then one guy drove while the other two pointed out the best route. Look, if we have to, we'll carry our gear by hand and just bulldog our bikes through," he paused again. "C'mon, it's not supposed to be easy!"

"Right now the Sahara seems like a nice warm place to be!" said Jeff.

Kacie had a sly grin on her face. "Bit like Mexico eh!"

PJ looked around at everyone. "I dunno guys. What do you reckon? I don't want to go back to the cabin." Jeff and Mike were not looking very happy.

"Shit," said Mike. That about summed everything up. There was another short silence.

"Riding the bikes loaded like this is gay," said Kacie. "But we have to do it."

"Yes," agreed PJ. "They're handling like crap, I just about lost it several times already. The rear end of my Gasser keeps stepping out on me in the corners."

"They do that on the tarseal don't they," said Jeff, grinning. PJ usually beat him in Trials so he enjoyed times like this when

PJ was at a disadvantage.

PJ grinned back at Jeff, he liked a challenge. “Bloody Trials tyres are a pain on tarseal. Even pumped up they let go if you corner too hard. They chunk too. Throw the centre treads. Looks scary when you see it. I’m not going to get more than four or five days out my rear tyre. Probably run out of gas before then anyway.”

“With your tank, *you will*! Then we’ll have to help you!” Jeff said in a sing-song voice. Jeff was loving this!

Mike turned to Kacie. “Are you sure you want to take this logging road?”

The bridge at Boston Bar

Kacie looked him in the eyes. “Yes, I’m sure. If PJ can do it in his pickup then so can we on the bikes.” Kacie was a fantastic Trials rider. Better than all of them put together.

PJ looked pleased. “Once we get across the bridge, we have to follow the railway line north about ten maybe fifteen miles then we head west up a valley.”

And that was it. They said goodbye and good luck to the family in the Dodge van and headed off south to cross the Fraser river at Boston Bar. As they crossed the bridge PJ had the feeling of being watched. He looked back and on either side but saw nothing, yet still this was not a nice feeling to have. It usually meant someone nasty was staring at you and thinking bad things.

Black rocks and meltwater

The tarseal ended a few miles on the other side of the town, then there was about ten miles of easy riding on a good fire road before it headed west inland and got a little rougher. The track scrambled up and down hills and followed a small river with big black rocks and wildly tumbling melt water for another seven miles. Then there were two major splits at three valleys. They veered left at the first valley after crossing a log bridge, and then a few hundred yards later left again across another log bridge towards a smaller valley. They stopped while PJ checked his map. "We have to go south here."

Mike looked at him. "Are you sure?"

"Yep. I remember it real well. The whole detour is about 60 miles, give or take."

Mike was not very happy; everyone could see that, but none of them were sure of anything anymore—so no one said anything. They trusted PJ. So far he had been right.

While they were stopped PJ looked back down the road. "I thought I heard an engine." Everyone listened. There was nothing. "Maybe it's my imagination. Anyone else have the feeling of being watched when we crossed the bridge back at Boston Bar?"

"Yes," said Kacie. "I thought it was just me."

Mike was looking nervously back down the road. "You think we're being followed?"

"I hope not. I don't hear it any more. Ahh, maybe I was imagining it."

Now they headed south on a smaller and less travelled logging road. The road had been climbing steadily up to the point where they took the valley to the south. Now it got steeper. The thick moss on the rocks under the huge firs started to disappear as they went up in altitude. So far the bridges they had come to had all been in good condition and these forestry roads were real easy to ride on the trail bikes, even as heavily loaded as they were. The bridges were built to carry loaded logging trucks so they were going to last for a long time.

The smaller road

They made a pee stop, and as they were getting back on the bikes they heard a chilling sound from way below them in the valley back the way they had come. It was faint but unmistakably the sound of a V8 engine with a noisy after market exhaust. They all listened looking down the road as panic started to set in and their nerves took on an edge. “Hey guys. C’mon, lets go, it’s real. We got someone coming after us,” said PJ talking very quickly. So the four of them got their bikes fired up and took off as fast as possible. Now the road became pretty steep and they came to the worst slide area: two places where there was barely room for a four-wheeler. Lots of sharp jagged rock on the side and a long way to fall if you slipped over the edge. “This was the worst bit,” shouted PJ. “We’re lucky it’s still OK. Pity, but it’s not going to stop a four wheeler.”

“You remember where the slides were?” Kacie shouted back.

“I’ve a pretty good memory for places I’ve been to in the bundu, and a fairly good sense of direction, I don’t always get it right though. Huh, this probably isn’t the time to say that!”

The rock slide area

About five miles further on they were up around three thousand feet; all around them parts of the hills on either side had been clear-cut by the loggers and there were blackened stumps and the burnt remains of the logging. It didn't look too good. Now they came to a fairly big washout across the road. It was just after a small logging road took off left up the side of the valley. Run off from the stream beside the side road had caused it.

PJ glanced up the small logging road and saw what looked like a pretty severe gap about a half mile up. "You guys get through here, don't leave any tyre tracks and head on up the road to where you can see this. Stay out of sight. I'm going to lead whatever's after us up that logging road and try and lose them or get them stuck. I'll make my way back and catch up with you."

Everyone was frozen as if in a trance just watching PJ, not knowing quite what to do. "Go-on, MOVE!"

Everyone snapped out of it and moved but Kacie stayed with PJ. "I'm going to give you a hand."

PJ took one glance at the determined look on her face and nodded his head. "OK." They both uncoupled the spare gas cans from round their waists and stashed them and their packs and their other spare gas cans on the far side of the washout out of sight. As they got back on their bikes the others were disappearing around a turn about a mile up the road. They rode back and turned up the small logging road until they were almost out of sight round a bend and stopped.

They didn't have long to wait. They heard the vehicle before it appeared. It was a chilling sound, not going fast but coming closer with a confidence based on being the biggest and meanest sons of bitches on the block. Then it came into sight: it was a big black late model pickup with oversize mud tyres. It had what the Aussies call a "Bull bar" on the front, with a winch built in, and a heavy duty roll bar over the cab. There were several powerful lights both on the roll bar and hanging on the Bull bar. It looked like there were three men in the cab. They saw PJ and Kacie and the two of them gassed it, kicking up the dirt as they spun their rear tyres and headed quickly up the small logging road. The road zig-zagged up the side of a large clear-cut. Looking back they could see the pickup had taken the bait and was following them about two zigs behind. The road had been partially undercut at a U-bend in a gully which the two bikes had no trouble with but when they looked back as they got further on they could see the pickup had stopped and the two passengers were inspecting the washout. PJ and Kacie stopped and watched as the pickup backed up and then made a dash at the washout. Amazingly it was able to use the camber of the U-bend as a berm and made it with its front wheels up the other side. The two of them got going again as the passengers started pushing the pickup to get the back wheels up on to the road.

About a half mile later they got to the end of the road. Ahead was the forest and there was just the usual mess of stumps and small logs and branches on either side of the road in the clear-cut. "Now we'll see who can go off road and whose just play-acting," PJ said.

They both took off through the jumble of brush and stumps, heading almost straight downhill towards where the main road was way below them at the bottom of the valley. It was really tricky riding through this stuff even though it was down hill. Kacie's extra riding skill meant she had about the same trouble riding her trail bike as PJ had on his competition trials bike. They both had to paddle like crazy in places putting their feet down every which way to get the bikes over the small logs and branches and general mess left behind by the logging. The metal pipe that held the extra gas cans on the side of the engine really got in the way of their legs. It was tiring and required intense concentration. But then PJ got his front wheel tucked under as he went over a log and the bike sent him over the bars and then landed on top of him. Both his legs were trapped and his body was upside-down facing downhill. The bike was revving it's heart out and there was absolutely no way for him to pull his legs out from under it. Kacie was off her bike in a flash, and took off her left glove as she ran over. Then she used her left glove as a pad underneath her right hand and slammed it over the end of the exhaust to kill the engine. Then she lifted the bike up enough so that PJ could get his legs free.

"Are you OK?" she asked.

PJ got on his feet, pushed his bike upright and wiped some dirt off the handgrips and his gloves. "I'm fine. Thanks, good job you were here!"

Kacie grinned. "Well this was important, I didn't want to

leave it just to a man!"

They both laughed and high-fived. The two of them fired up their bikes and carried on down the hill. The pickup meanwhile was out of the gully with the washout and racing up the road. It stopped when it got to the end of the road and all three men got out and stood looking down at them bushwhacking their way back to the forestry road at the bottom.

"They were tricking us, and now the bastards are getting away!" said one of the men. "Let's go get the fuckers!" They ran back to the pickup, turned it round and tore off back down the road. When they got to the washout at the U-bend in the gully they were not so careful this time and the driver charged at it thinking speed would get him across. It didn't, and the pickup slipped down into the gully and rolled over on to its roof.

When they got to the bottom and back on the main forestry road PJ and Kacie could see the three men trying to push the pickup back on its wheels in the gully. They put the cans back on either side of the engine, shouldered their packs, strapped the spare gas cans to their waists and headed off to join Mike and Jeff up ahead. They found them waiting out of sight just round the bend in the road. "They have a winch," said PJ, "but it's still going to take them best part of an hour or two to get out of that gully and come after us."

"I think it will take them longer than that," said Kacie.

"Let's hope so," said Jeff.

A further eight or nine miles and they were up at four thousand feet and there were mostly evergreen firs. There were some spectacular open rock faces and cliffs and also the occasional non-fir tree whose autumn colours were matched by large numbers of red berries on tiny plants growing close to the ground.

Colourful leaves

As well there were colourful swaths of red and yellow leaves on other small bushes everywhere in the open where the forest had been logged. Despite the logging it was still a beautiful sight. It was so nice to look around and realise that those were not telephone poles in the distance but solitary dead trees. Up above the slopes of the valley they were in they could see ominous signs of snow on the next range of hills. A few miles further the grade started going down.

The top of the switchback

“That’s it guys, we’re about half way, it’s all downhill now!” PJ wasn’t far wrong. The road was dropping quite steeply now and they went down a switchback with a scary looking drop off on the right. There were several slides here that had been cleared not long ago.

It was a good feeling heading downhill; somehow it felt like the worst was over...

Chapter 4, Harrison Lake.

Ahead of them they could see some tall mountains covered in snow, part of the Coast Mountains they were passing through. It wouldn't be long before snow blanketed everything around here and shut this forestry track down.

Jeff looked up at the snow in the distance. "Our timing is pretty good so far guys."

About ten miles later they turned left where another valley with a logging road on it headed north. Now they were going almost directly south with a river way below them in a deep gorge to their left. They had dropped low enough in altitude that the thick moss was back under the trees. The branches of the trees

The high bridge

and bushes leaned out into the track making them dodge and weave to avoid them. It wasn't going to take long before the forest reclaimed this road completely.

They crossed a bridge over the gorge that had no guard rails, with the river tumbling and rushing about eighty feet below them. Then they went another hour or so and the track they were on flattened out.

"We're pretty close to the lake here," said PJ. A few more miles and peeking through the trees they could see the now placid river opening out just a bit.

First view of the lake

"It's Harrison Lake!" sad PJ triumphantly. They could hardly wait but it was still several miles before they were finally at the lake shore. The forest opened up into a logging camp at the lakes edge. They rode through what they thought was the abandoned work site towards the beach, past some logging equipment, and then got off and stretched.

Just then they heard dogs, and a man with the wildest look upon his face appeared around a large pile of logs on the other side of the clearing. He had long unkempt hair, and five of the biggest, meanest dogs they had ever seen. PJ waved at the man and smiled, but the man's response was to let loose the dogs, and howling for blood they streaked towards the friends.

The logging camp

"Geezus!" exclaimed Jeff.

"Let's go!" yelled PJ. "Go! Get the hell out of here!" They got on the bikes, kicked them into life, and headed towards the pack rushing at them. The dogs were between them and the way south. PJ was first and he aimed his Gasser directly at the lead animal. He slipped the clutch and revved the engine, then dropped the clutch. This popped his front wheel about a foot in the air, launching himself over the beast and sending it careening into the dog behind. The two dogs tumbled over each other out of control. Jeff was headed to the right of the pack and attracted the biggest one of all. As the animal lunged at his left leg, he swung it back and buried his hiking boot in the jaws of the huge beast. There was a prototype snarl in the animal's mouth that was cut short into a quickly smothered yelp as its head snapped back and the animal was bowled over. The other two beasts were confused by all the bikes streaming by them, and by the time they had turned round and figured out who to go for everyone had passed and was well out of reach.

The friends didn't stop any time soon. They slid round corners, lofted their front wheels over rocks and potholes, and sped down the straights. About eight miles further on they came to a nice picnic spot on the waters edge, so they pulled over and parked the bikes. There was no sound of the dogs in pursuit. Jeff and PJ were laughing and even Mike had a grin on his face.

"Are we safe here?" said Kacie.

"I reckon," said PJ. "This is way out of their territory. They won't bother us now. Man, I laid the lead dog out. Just smushed the bastard."

"Yeah, and one of those suckers is going to have trouble chewing!" said Jeff. "I guess that bloke was the caretaker."

Mike had a smile on his face. "Nice guy, huh!"

Jeff was staring out across the water, back the way they had come. "I wonder what he's saving it for?"

"How about a nice cup of tea?" suggested Kacie.

"That sounds real good," said PJ.

Jeff looked around at the picnic area. "We should think about camping for the night before we get back to the main roads. Right here would be pretty good. What do you reckon guys?"

"Here would be good to camp," agreed PJ. "We've still got about ten miles to go before we're back on tarseal at the township. The track more or less follows the lake shore all the way."

Mike looked around and nodded his head. "Yeah. We can leave early and be at the bridge over the Fraser before anyone wakes up. If there is anyone."

"I'm good with that," said Kacie.

The camp site at Harrison Lake

They moved the bikes to where they couldn't be seen from the road, and prepared a campfire close to the shore on the other side of a bunch of big old dry logs that had been washed up high by storm waves. It was pleasant on the lake shore. There was no breeze and lots of dry bleached driftwood to cook with and warm them up late into the night.

"I stopped here when I came through in my pickup. Took a bunch of nice photos to jog my memory when I wrote it up." PJ paused and took a sip of tea. "Strange how things change, all my stories are gone now. Sitting there on the hard drive at home. Guess it doesn't really matter, just the same as dying. Nothing matters any more when you die. All your stories end then."

Driftwood at the camp site

"Yeah, well our stories are not ending now," said Kacie with a smile.

The fire had died down into embers as they lay snuggled up in their sleeping bags... when lights appeared flickering through the trees heading towards them from back the way they had come.

PJ looked intensely at the lights. "Bet it's those guys that were chasing us; they won't see the fire, they'll drive right on by."

"Bloody hell, I hope you're right," said Mike. They all got their bows ready.

"We'll take them out if they do come for us," said Jeff. "They won't expect us to be armed."

"They won't stop," said PJ. "They won't see us. They have a string of high powered lights on the road and their vision will be virtually nil outside of that."

"They'll be hungry and just looking to go home," Kacie said. "They don't *want* to see us."

"Good point," Mike agreed. "I wouldn't mind going home right now either!"

It was quite scary watching the lights get closer and closer with the sound of the V8 fading up and down as the road dipped through denser patches of trees and in and out of small inlets on the lake shore. Then as the V8 growl hit a crescendo the pickup tooled right on by and never even looked like stopping.

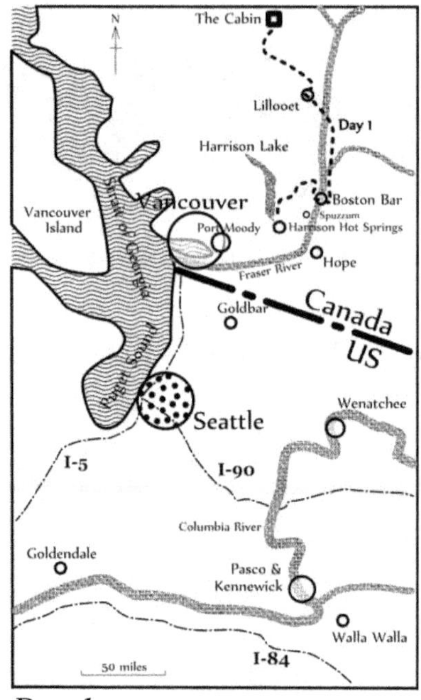

Day 1

"Wow," exclaimed Jeff. "Guess you two were right."

"I wonder if those guys have something to do with the roadblock at Hope?" remarked PJ.

"Let's hope not, then maybe they'll get shot up if they go back that way!" answered Kacie.

"Ooh, I didn't know you were like that!" said PJ.

"Oh there's some things you really don't want to know about me," replied Kacie with a wicked grin.

Mike got up and placed some big logs on the fire so it would last the night. There was silence as each of them looked at the remains of the fire, then so quickly the dark starlight and glowing red embers worked their ancient magic and they slept.

The next morning they headed out while it was still dark, but light enough that they could travel without using their lights. The air was super cold next to the lake and even though they were riding slowly the wind they made as they travelled chilled their hands and faces. Pretty soon not just their fingers and hands but their entire bodies felt frozen. Just before they got to the township of Harrison Hot Springs at the southern edge of the lake they stopped near the shore, holding their gloved hands on the hot engines and stomping around trying to get warm.

Jeff was stamping his feet and swinging his arms from side to side. "That's the thing about riding a motorcycle. No matter how warm you dress you only lose heat and you get colder. There's just not enough energy expended by your body to replace what you lose."

Harrison Lake from the access road

"More clothes just delays the inevitable," added PJ. "Sooner or later you freeze your butt off!"

"Damn it's cold!" said Kacie.

They passed through the township without incident and made their way down through the streets of Agassiz to the Fraser River, but found the approach causeway to the bridge had been blocked with burned-out vehicles. There had obviously been a major tidal surge up the river even though they were about 50 miles inland. Driftwood and other debris was laying everywhere. Most of the trees were down and all the buildings were flattened. They stopped and looked for a way through but it was pretty hopeless.

"Looks like this was blocked on purpose," said Mike.

"Probably to get any travellers to go through the roadblock at Hope," said PJ.

"We'll have to try Mission," suggested Jeff. "I sure hope the bridge there is OK."

"It's our last best chance," agreed Kacie. "The other bridges out of Vancouver are supposed to have road blocks. We're not going to get through them."

So they backtracked and headed south on the Lougheed Highway. Large parts of this road were on flood plains and low lying. It had all been under water and the farmland and crops were pretty much wiped out. It was a bit tricky in places where water had sluiced the road away but they were able to make it through by walking their gear over and then man-handling the bikes across.

"That family we met up by Boston Bar must have had trouble here," said PJ.

There was heavy fog coming off the Fraser River as they approached Mission. It was still very early in the morning and they were right up on the bridge before they could see it was open. As they crossed the bridge the fog was real good to be in because it muffled the sound of the bikes and made them feel invisible. It was a straight shot down through Abbotsford and across what had once been the border with the US. Now it was just another collection of derelict buildings. There had been some serious flooding here too. Part of the tidal wave that had apparently swept through and obliterated Richmond and other parts of the Lower Mainland and had made a real mess of things.

They could see a string of large concrete blocks and a swinging pipe barrier across the road right about where the border had been. They stopped and looked but nothing moved. They rode closer and Jeff went ahead and stopped at the barrier. It was locked but there was no one there so he motioned the others to come. They laid each bike on its side and dragged it under the pole and rode on.

So far that day they hadn't seen anyone else and it was only a matter of threading their way past all the rubbish and abandoned vehicles on the roads. PJ had his collection of maps with him, with the current one in a clear plastic bag taped on top of the gear bag strapped on to his handlebars. He had always had an aversion to satellite controlled navigation systems.

Kacie looked at the route they were taking on the map. “Just as well you’ve got these. There’s no GPS up there telling us where to go now.”

They kept away from I-5 because they had heard reports it was totally blocked and impassible, travelling instead on the smaller highway through Sedro Woolley, bypassing Mt. Vernon. PJ was checking his radiation meter every time they stopped now and the level was slowly getting higher.

The small road was twisting and winding its way through all the lush green valleys of this part of Washington and they had no major trouble until they got close to Highway 2. Nearing the highway the road was totally blocked by a semi that had hit a four wheeler. On the other side of the semi the road was a parking lot full of abandoned vehicles, mostly cars and pickups with some SUV’s upside down or on their sides or bogged up to their axles in the grass and mud off on the side of the road. With the bikes they managed to keep going by squeezing through small spaces between the vehicles and by taking to the dirt and grass on the verge and motocrossing their way through. Then they headed east on Highway 2.

As they made their way through the wreckage on the road heading towards Monroe it was like a disease had blighted the buildings, in pockets though, burning only some to the ground. In these places just concrete and brick fireplaces were left, with concrete stairways leading to where the front and back doors had been. Other areas were OK, and looked normal except for the overgrown gardens. None of the friends felt at ease and the men in particular kept looking out for trouble coming at them. Even though nothing happened, it was still creepy.

Monroe was a real mess; there had been some nasty fighting there as people tried to flee the remains of Seattle. There were only three ways out of Seattle: North, South and East. South was completely blocked by lahars (mud and boulder slides) from an earthquake that triggered a small eruption of Mt. Rainier. There were only two routes East. Highway 2 through Monroe was the smaller one. Not that it made any difference if you had six lanes or two. Tens of thousands of vehicles wouldn't fit on a hundred lanes. Not all at one time anyway. In the panic filled and half-dark days of smoke and dust and chaos, with the full-on deep, dark and murderous night, and on foot eventually: most everyone died. Near as makes no difference. No matter what the poets said, we were still animals at heart.

Now the four of them had to make a decision to stick with Highway 2 or try to make it to I-90 along the foothills of the Cascade mountains. The radiation had been ramping up on the way south down to Highway 2 and then it had stayed pretty much the same level all the way to Monroe.

PJ looked at his radiation meter. "It's probably going to go higher if we head south from here and try to use I-90 and Snoqualmie Pass. We should take 2 and go through Wenatchee. Besides, that way we can check on Tim at his place near Moses Lake." Tim and his wife Julie were part of the eastern Washington Trials scene and had a good looking daughter named Wendy.

"You wouldn't be thinking about Wendy would you," asked Mike with a smile on his face. Everyone grinned and Kacie poked PJ in the side with her finger as he tried not to look embarrassed!

"Just a thought!" said PJ.

Chapter 5, Goldbar.

The centre of Monroe was bad with the highway like the parking lot at the wreckers yard but they got through using the back alleys and side streets. Just after the town Highway 2 was choked by abandoned and burnt out vehicles and littered with the remains of corpses. 4×4's had tried to get through on the edges of the road and across the fields on either side, eventually bogging each other down until there was nowhere else to go. On the bikes they had better luck riding along the rail line between the road and the river although the sleepers pounded the hell out of both them and the bikes. It was like riding a high speed pile-driver on a pebble beach, tricky too, keeping between the rails without losing your balance.

PJ glanced back at everyone following. "Glad we don't have to worry about meeting a train!"

The Celestial Coffeehouse

They were able to get back on the road at Sultan because so few people had made it that far and the road was clear again.

Sultan had partially burned but the next village of Startup was one of those places that was still standing although the river had overflowed at some point and there was a huge log-jam they had to bypass just before they got into the village. They knew this road well from back when they rode Trials at Goldbar. They would stop and have a meal in the little eating places that had grown up over the generations in these tiny villages. It was a bummer but they weren't going to be meeting their friends for a weekend's riding over the slippery moss covered rocks in the woods near Goldbar any more. The Barbecue Pit at Startup had been a good place to eat a meal with your mates. You could order anything you liked but there really wasn't any point in eating at the Barbecue Pit if you didn't order ribs! The small cottage style building was still there but it was called the Celestial Coffeehouse now and covered with stars and moons and suns... and darkness inside the windows.

At Goldbar they stopped for a break and emptied the last of the gas in the gas cans balanced on their tanks into the tanks themselves. PJ disappeared off on the other side of the railway tracks to "Pay my respects to my ancestors!" When they were all ready to ride again PJ was patting down his pockets. "I must have left my Swiss Army knife back in the bush, I was cutting my fingernails. Damn. You guys carry on. I'll be right with you." So the other three rode off while PJ walked back to pick up his knife.

The 'Rest stop' at Goldbar

As the three left Goldbar there was an unmanned barricade across the road so they rode past it on a small path through the grass and dirt on the side of the road. Then as they went by the firehall and up the small rise on the other side of Reiter road, half a dozen men carrying guns and rifles rushed out of a building that had been a restaurant and stood by the barricade looking at them disappearing up the road. Just then PJ came into view behind them and as the sound of the two-stroke reached the men they swung round and one put a shotgun up to his shoulder. Their leader put his hand out and swung the barrel down. “No shooting, We’re going to have us some fun!”

They all whooped and hollered and rushed over to where there were a couple of heavily modified four by fours with giant wheels and tyres: rock crawlers. The noise as the V8 engines in these huge beasts crackled and rumbled into life was monstrous. They spun their tyres in the dust on the side of the road and laid rubber on the tarseal as they screeched off down the road towards PJ.

As PJ saw them he said “Fuck!” He didn’t swear often, but this was the right word for the job! He slammed on the brakes and spun round in the dirt on the side of the road. Barrelling back down the road he searched his memory banks for a way out. May Creek road miraculously popped up. He had heard the local Trials guys talking about riders who had gotten lost and ended up having to use May Creek road to get back to the parking lot at Goldbar. PJ guessed it went right by where they rode Trials in the park, but how did he get to May Creek road? The next major junction was with 1st so he turned off there and headed north.

The others rode on for about five miles then stopped and

waited for PJ. "He must have had a problem finding his knife," said Mike. Jeff and Kacie were looking a little bit nervous.

"You don't think he had trouble at the roadblock?" asked Kacie. They stopped their engines and sat there on the bikes, looking back down the empty road.

Heading north on 1st, PJ was riding as fast as the little Gas Gas would go, about 55mph. He reached over with his left hand and squeezed the clip on the belt holding the big gas can on top of the bike's gas tank. The plastic can was now empty as he had already transferred everything to his bike's tank, and it tumbled and bounced away behind him followed by the big red belt that had held it to his waist. About half a mile later there was May Creek road crossing 1st. "Yeah, baby!" thought PJ. So he took off right, then about a mile and a half later he turned left down a small road past a whole bunch of "Private Property. Do Not Enter signs" and dodged into the forest on the western edge of where they had ridden Trials.

The track he was on got really rough and then it dipped down and crossed May Creek. There was two or three feet of rushing water in places. He chose what looked like the shallowest spot but had to use all of his Trials skills to keep the bike moving and avoid being thrown sideways as the water upstream pressed and tumbled against his wheels. If he slipped the bike would be submerged and the chances were the engine would suck water in through the air filter and die. After some really intense moments he got across without falling. "Phew!" he said to himself.

Immediately he had to concentrate again because the other side of the creek was really rough with loose rocks, logs, boulders, and big holes carved out by flood water. His experience all over the world doing stupid things on motorcycles really helped. He attacked all this seemingly impassible jumble with the vigour and urgency of just one more life or death struggle on the road; amongst all the others he had had to deal with. And it worked. A series of intense moves later with big throttle followed by short bursts of trailing or no throttle, plus strategically placed feet down on the rocks or logs, and finally he made the last scramble up the other side. With the back tyre spitting rocks and dirt behind him in a rooster tail and more than a hint of panic thumping in his heart, he found his way through the trees to where the track opened up and became a regular fire road again.

Trashing the riding area

Just then he heard the 4×4's as they churned up the water and rocks in the creek. "Damn, they're still on my trail." So PJ got on the gas and tore off down the dirt road. There were big puddles of muddy water across the whole road which he skirted round the edge going as fast as he dared, right up to the bushes and trees overhanging the road. When he got to where they used to camp he kept on left at the Y junction, because heading out of the riding area from here would mean the 4×4's would catch him as they would be much faster once they got back on to the tarseal of Reiter road. There was some small brush littered on the fire road from wind storms which he easily got by but he knew it wouldn't slow the chasing vehicles either. This riding area had been closed down for many years now because of the damage done by "ripper" or "rat" bikes (old junk dirt bikes) and drunken louts in pickups. The pickups stayed in the open areas and trashed those places while the rat bikes really made a mess of the trails mostly because of their big open knobby tyres coupled with way too much power for the average Joe. The combination of the knobby tyres, overpowered engines and riders with no skill meant these bikes just ripped their way into the dirt and dug huge holes. Most of the guys that rode these bikes didn't have a clue how to get traction, and balance to them was something you did so you didn't spill your beer.

Traction is one thing that is a speciality of Trials riders, traction and balance. If you're good at Trials you can practically float over and through the gnarliest of terrain leaving a relatively small footprint behind. But it takes time, skill and really hard work to get good at Trials. That rules out 90% of all motorcycle riders. Of course the major thing against Trials for most people is that it's a sport that has no racing and no speed.

PJ had a plan... if he carried on along this fire road he would get to a turn off to the right about a half-mile further. That would lead back on a track so rough the crawler's speed would be reduced to slower than a walking pace where the track crossed some huge open boulders for about 100 feet. But first he was going to lead them the wrong way. He passed the place they called "three-step", three big rock steps that they used for Trials sections long ago. But too steep for him to go down with his bike still laden with gas cans on the side and a rather cumbersome pack on his back. He got to the junction and headed left for a couple of hundred feet, then turned off the road up the bank at the start of one of the old Trials loop trails. This trail led up the hill to the north side of the riding area. His plan was to get hidden, let the crawlers go past and then head out back to the other road, over the exposed rocks and out of the off-road riding area. But as he got a few feet into the trees he fell off on some tree roots and stalled the engine. This was it; too late for anything else now!

He was panicking and half way through picking the bike up when he heard the sound of the rock crawlers. Rurr-rurr-rurr-rurr. A deep menacing rumble that absolutely chilled his blood. PJ froze with the bike half-way up holding it in tension as the two vehicles went slowly right on by, their huge power even at idling revs able to take them up the road with ease. The men were sitting on the backs of the seats and hanging on to the big roll bars. They had bandanna and cowboy hats over their heads, and assault rifles by their sides. No one-eyed bearded pirates of old could have looked more menacing. They weren't even rushing, no need to; they knew they were the big boss hogs in this game.

As they disappeared up the road the biggest guy there, a huge bear of a man, swung his head sideways as if he had caught a glimpse in his mind's eye of where PJ was. He put his rifle down on the floor and slipped quietly off the side of the last crawler. Then he stood there, half crouching, hidden in the foliage on the edge of the road about 50 feet out of sight of PJ. PJ got his bike up and pushed it back down towards the track. He listened, still hidden in the trees until the sound of the crawlers had gone. Now he fired up his Gasser and headed out of the trees and down the bank. As he did this the bear of a man broke cover and ran at him uttering a huge roar. The surprise was so great for PJ that he just about freaked out of his mind. But his lifetime of competition experience triggered him to gas it; he dropped the clutch and slid the bike sideways on the road, short-shifting all the way to 5th with the engine wailing and the man in hot pursuit. Then PJ hit 6th gear and tapped the bike out.

The open rock area

The man soon gave up, it didn't take him long to realise he didn't have a chance of catching the bike now that it was up to speed. He had been drinking and although he was big and strong he was way out of condition for running. PJ didn't look back and rode as if a real bear was on his tail. Just like when racing he never looked back when he was in the lead. Looking back only slowed you down. The little Gas Gas had disappeared from sight down the other road by the time the crawlers returned. The "Bear" climbed his way back on board and their leader signalled everyone to cut their engines. In the silence heading down the other fire road they could hear the two stroke getting fainter all the time, the engine revs going up and down as PJ rode through the mud holes and dodged the small tree-falls. The leader got everyone going again. "C'mon I think I know where he's headin'. We can get through there and still catch him."

PJ was approaching the very rough patch of open rock, the other side of which led to the access road and then out onto Reiter road. The open rock was quite tricky with his heavily laden bike but he managed not to fall off as he crossed the fissures and cracks dug into the surface of the rock. A hundred feet later, he hung a left off the track into the forest on what was now a disused four wheel drive track. He knew it had been used in Trials when it was a game trail a bunch of years ago and it would let him cut directly onto the entrance access road. The crawlers could follow him but at least they wouldn't be any faster.

The four wheel drive trail

One place had a big fallen tree completely blocking the track so PJ broke right into the bush and had to apply all his skill and concentration to get through the bottom of a gully and up the other side amongst the trees and roots and rocks. He paused slightly at the bottom to look carefully at the worst bit of the uphill part, got third gear and then he wound on the gas just enough to launch the bike up and over the top. As he rocketed up he cut the throttle and momentarily pulled the clutch in so the back wheel would not spin or skip sideways. While he was doing this his momentum carried him up over the bad stuff. This was basic Trials technique, but done now with an urgency that gave his every move a precision that would have given him top honours in a competition. But there were no observers to pass score and no spectators to see and applaud. This wasn't just extreme riding, this was riding like he used to do in East Africa in the Great Rift Valley and the jungles on the lower slopes of Mt. Kilimanjaro and Mt. Kenya. This was riding in the raw.

Reiter road

Once he got back on the other side of the downed tree it was only a few hundred yards until he got to Reiter road. There was a locked forestry gate that hadn't been there before, but he was able to wriggle his way past on the right hand side through the space between some big boulders that was just wide enough for his bike. The crawlers could never get through here, they would have to find another way out of the forest, "That should slow them down," said PJ grimly.

He turned right and sped flat out, through the tall dark firs standing right up to the edge and even partially into the narrow strip of tarseal. There was no safety net on this road. A bit like life in the wild, you really had to look out for yourself. No one was there to hold your hand and keep you out of trouble. Half a mile later at Highway 2 he hung a left and pinned the throttle heading up towards Skykomish. He looked back to see if the road was still clear. There was no one behind him. So far so good.

Highway 2 heading towards Skycomish

Kacie, Mike and Jeff had just made up their minds to go back and look for PJ when they saw him: a cloud of blue smoke hauling ass towards them. They paused for a brief moment and then they all realised something was terribly wrong. PJ never went flat out, none of them did, they were trying to save gas! "Let's get out of here," shouted Jeff.

The three of them fired up their bikes and were almost up to cruising speed when PJ went by signalling and shouting to them all to "Get on it!" They raced through Skykomish on Highway 2 and up the long sweeping curves of the 4000 foot climb to the top of Stevens Pass.

Snow on the summit of Stevens Pass

There were two or three inches of snow for about half a mile either side of the summit, so the four of them spread out and rode in their own virgin part of the road. The first snow of winter was always fun to play in but this was not play time; there was some real urgency now.

This was life and death time.

Chapter 6, Friends!

As the crawlers got to the top of Stevens Pass, they stopped and the leader got out and looked at the four motorcycle tracks in the snow twisting and sliding their way into the distance. “Waal, we sure had fun. Those asshole bikers ain’t coming back on *our* road!” And the crawlers went back down to get them some more booze in their broken little town at the bottom of the valley.

For the four friends it was only a short way down the other side of Stevens Pass before the road was clear of snow and it was Autumn again, but the slopes a little higher on either side of the valley had a blanket of snow underneath the trees. This was not going to be a good place to travel very shortly.

Autumn on the other side of Stevens Pass

When they got to the junction with highway 97 they carried on through Wenatchee. They had dropped their speed back down to normal by now figuring the crawlers weren’t going to chase them this far. It would be good to see their friends on the farm again and even if they weren't there it would be a safe place to spend the night. The roads were pretty much clear on this side of the mountains so they made good time, stopping to stretch their legs where the Columbia River made a huge bow a few miles the other side of Wenatchee. They could see a mile or so back the way they had come but the road stayed empty behind them. They were overlooking the river in a big open area that had scattered rocks, dry grass and a few small scrubby bushes. "Nice place for a picnic," said Jeff. "Who was supposed to bring the beer?"

"I thought it was you!" said Mike.

"Maybe Tim will have beer... and that's the real reason for calling by his place!" said PJ.

"I thought you didn't drink," said Kacie.

"Oh there are times when I make an exception," said PJ with a slight smile.

"I've seen you have a beer," said Jeff.

"Yeah, but only one, and it wasn't this year!"

The bow in the Columbia river near Wenatchee

It took another few hours travelling on the deserted roads before they pulled up into Tim's spread with plenty of light left in the day. Tim and Wendy and two other woman were there to meet them and they all had rifles in their hands. Out in the country down here everyone had guns.

They lowered their rifles when they saw who it was and Tim started off by telling them that he didn't know what had happened to his wife Julie. She had been in Spokane visiting her parents but when Tim went looking for her, there was nothing, just an empty house where her parents had lived. They all said sorry but that's really all you can say.

Kacie went up to Wendy and hugged her and then kissed Tim on the cheek and hugged him. Wendy introduced Marie and her daughter Sandy. They were friends who had been visiting them on the farm when everything blew up. Marie was a veterinarian in her late forties, while Sandy was twenty years younger and into real estate. Both of them were part of the eastern Washington Trials scene and pretty fair riders.

PJ shook Tims hand and said sorry about his wife, then somewhat awkwardly held out his hand to Wendy realizing too late that she was expecting a hug, so there was one of those little oh-darn-what-do-I-do-now dances from both of them which ended as a rather half hearted shake of the hand, when both of them would have preferred a hug.

Tim was 43, about five foot eight with a stocky build; he had a square-jawed face and was tough and weather-beaten like most farmers. He had a quick wit which he delivered with a deadpan look on his face that slowly changed to a big grin when the effect had been achieved and had a laconic almost southern drawl although he was native to eastern Washington. Tim had been a good Trials rider on the local scene when he was in his thirties but now he spent most of his time working on the farm, only occasionally riding events.

Tim's daughter Wendy was 26, tall and good-looking like her

mum. Like her dad she was tough but unlike her dad she was a talented Trials rider, even getting good enough to ride Expert on the national level at one point in time—in fact one of the best woman riding Trials in North America.

"What sort of trouble did you guys have getting here?" asked Tim.

"Vancouver has a bunch of roadblocks, we had to make a big detour through Harrison Lake," said PJ, "and there was one in Goldbar that I didn't get through. I was a bit behind everyone so I led those bastards on their huge four by fours all through the worst trails I could remember. I ended up at the open rocks the other side of Three Step. I'm betting they had some trouble there!"

"What he means is he's so slow these guys chased his ass and bloody near caught him!" said Jeff.

Everyone laughed!

"Apparently they were killing people at the roadblocks in Vancouver," said Mike. "Women and children."

"The roads the other side of Stevens Pass are a real mess and blocked with wrecks," added Kacie. "We got through OK on the bikes."

"We had to ride a few miles on the railway between the rail lines just before Startup," said PJ. "The sleepers pounded the hell out of us!"

Kacie looked off into the distance. "The bodies are the worst thing though. The smell, you just have to close it off and not look, and ride by. There's nothing else to do. But even hours later when everything's long gone, you can't get the smell out of your nose."

"It's like the sight and smell is now a part of you," said Mike.

Tim had a bunch of trail bikes, mostly big single-banger four-strokes. He reckoned he could get them kitted up for the journey in two or three days. They weren't about to miss out on a trail ride to Mexico! Tim looked at PJ's Gas Gas and said "I know you don't like four strokes but why don't you take Julie's trail bike? It's an XT250 Yamaha. Way better for riding on the roads, and it's not bad on the dirt. We're just not going to be doing what your Gasser does best. Not any more. You can leave it here with our Trials bikes."

"Yeah, I hate four strokes but I guess it makes sense," said PJ. "What am I saying? I have to take it, my back tyre's starting to chunk its treads."

Wendy walked over and looked at the huge gaps in the tread on PJ's rear tyre. "Yeah, well you're not going much further on that baby!" Trials bikes have super grippy but very soft tyres and they don't last long on tarseal.

"It's a pity its a four-stroke," said PJ. "Noisy, heavy damn things! But I'll be real glad to get my backpack resting on something when I'm riding, my back's killing me!"

Wendy held out her hand and touched PJ on the arm. "We want you in good condition and good health, we need someone to follow when things get tough."

PJ smiled but didn't have the courage to put his hand out to her. "The XT will be just fine, my back will recover in a couple of days of not having to support the pack. I need to do some stretches."

He watched Wendy walk away and wished he was a bit more demonstrative. The awkwardness he felt being close to other people would change as the weeks passed and the trip south progressed. He would become much more natural as he adjusted to living in close contact with the others. But even with the closer physical space between them, he would maintain still some distance emotionally, though it would be less than before.

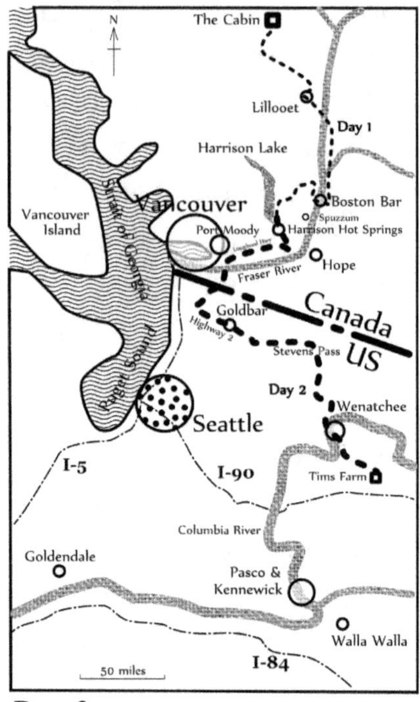

Day 2

Tim and Wendy had some hunting bows and packed those rather than their rifles. They could always make new arrows but when the ammo for the guns was gone they were just heavy bits of scrap metal. Marie and Sandy had only their rifles so they packed those. Tim topped them all up with gas from his pickup truck and his other farm vehicles and reckoned there should be a stash of gas near the border of Oregon with a friend. The longer they could ride the bikes, the better their chances of getting all the way south before winter. Their friend Dale was another farmer who had been a pretty fierce Trials competitor before he hurt his back taking a tumble at speed on the loop. It was a pleasant rest at Tim's farm and they stocked up on food for the road and did maintenance on the bikes. Three days later Tim had his bikes kitted out and they left.

The main highway through the cities of Pasco and Kennewick had a huge amount of wreckage and was a maze of crashed, burned out, and abandoned vehicles. After some bushwhacking they got through all right and crossed the Columbia river at Umatilla. It took them a few hours to get to Dale's farm way out off the beaten track in Oregon just south of Walla Walla. Dale had heard them coming and had a big grin on his face as they rode up.

"We thought we'd drop by to see if you could still ride a bike," said Tim in his southern drawl.

"Ride the pants off you!" retorted Dale with a fierce grin. Dale was in his mid-forties and was a redneck farmer from wayback. He hunted big game for sport, something Jeff had no time for. "The only reason to kill something is for food, or to defend yourself." But Dale sure had the kit. A thirty-ought six rifle with a scope and a large pair of binoculars as well. Deadly accurate stuff.

"Could be useful, I hear they have some pretty vicious gophers down in Mexico," drawled Tim. Everyone laughed!

Dale's farm

Like Tim, Dale had a stocky build but he was putting on extra pounds around his waist. Probably because he spent most of his day driving his huge do-it-all farm machine around his fields. "I bought the machine because it was cheaper than hiring people." Dale wasn't about to miss out on a trip to Mexico either. He had plenty of gas in his farm vehicles for them all and a big KTM trail bike which he kitted out with a couple of extra gas cans.

PJ explained their plans: "We're going to take I-84 west and then 97 south to Weed or thereabouts and then down I-5 until we find some place to dodge the radiation at LA."

"You don't want to head through Salt Lake City and go down inland?" asked Dale.

"No. I figure if we stay reasonably near the coast then if we have a bad spell of snow we have some chance of carrying on later when it clears. Inland it may never clear this close to winter."

"Yeah," said Dale, "could be. Guess it makes sense. Did any

place else get hit with nukes apart from LA?"

"Not the way we're going, as far as we know. But if LA's anything like Seattle the surrounding roads are going to be a real mess."

"What are we going to do long term?" said Dale.

"We haven't given it too much thought," said Kacie.

"Yeah, we've been concentrating on getting through one day at a time," added Mike.

"Ultimately we're going to have to walk," explained PJ, "and we're going to have to keep walking to get away from the extremes of heat and cold in summer and winter. So bring your best walking shoes."

"I've never been much into walking," mused Dale, "guess I don't have a choice now!"

"How's your back after that crash you had?" asked PJ.

"Oh I'm fine now," Dale replied, "takes more than that to put me down. Mind you I don't go quite so fast on the loop now. What sort of speed you guys going?"

"We're real slow," replied Kacie, "we're trying to save gas."

"Every mile we can get on the bikes is a huge bonus," said PJ.

"You can say that again," added Dale, "I really don't fancy walking over a thousand miles with a pack on my back!"

"We're all going to have to do that eventually," said PJ.

Dale just looked resigned and shook his head.

"By the way Dale you haven't got any seeds have you?" said PJ.

"Matter of fact I do, some Walla Walla sweet onions. I was going to give them to a hunting buddy in Colorado."

"I love Walla Walla sweet onions," said Kacie.

"Can't live without onions!" added Marie.

"Walla Walla ones are the best!" said Kacie.

"I got them from one of the Trials guys up in Walla Walla, so these are the real deal!"

"Anything else?" said PJ.

"Nope, my regular seeds are GM, I have to buy them every year."

"Ungh," said PJ in disgust.

"Fact of life in today's economy," added Dale.

"I'm sure glad we don't have to put up with that shit any more," said PJ.

While they were getting Dale's big KTM sorted out it was quite noticeable how Sandy looked worried and a bit miserable.

"What's up Sandy?" asked PJ.

Sandy perked up a bit as she responded to PJ's smile but shook her head indicating she didn't want to talk about it. Later PJ asked Marie and she replied that Sandy had been due to go in for an operation to remove a small tumour from one of her breasts when everything blew up with the world, so now she just had to live with it.

"Sometimes our bodies repair things like that," said PJ, "but you need the right mind-set and it's not something that your conscious brain can do. Having a good group of people around you helps."

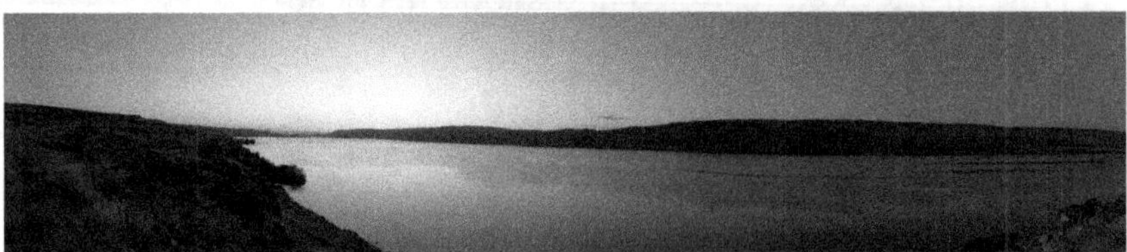

The Columbia river at dusk

They took off the next day in the late afternoon when Dale

had all his stuff together and they got to the Columbia River at dusk. They followed the river west and headed south on 97 at the bridge near Goldendale. It was dark as they went up the steep climb in the gorge that led onto the exposed open plateau above the southern side of the river. To their right was the Cascade Range and Mount Hood covered in snow and it was bone-chillingly cold on the bikes. They camped about 40 miles later after riding off the main road and finding a secluded and sheltered place. There they lit a fire and made some cocoa to warm them up before they went to bed.

"I'm going to miss my warm soft bed," said Dale.

"After a few days on the road," said Mike, "you'll be just fine."

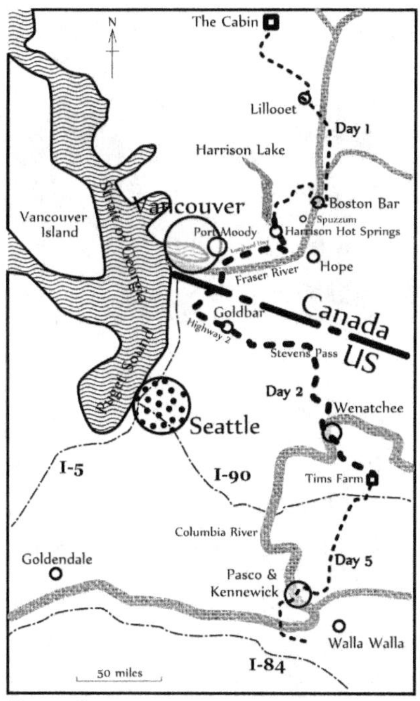

Day 5

Heather was hunting deer with her bow in the gorge when she heard the bikes. “Motorcycles? Heading up the gorge. What are they doing here?” Then for a brief moment she saw their headlights looking like a string of glow-worms floating up the road towards the plateau. Like she had been hit by lightning her whole body electrified as she realised what was going on. “They’re going south. Wait for me!” she yelled at the top of her voice and started running towards the road. “Wait! Wait! Please wait!” But it was too late. By the time she got there and stumbled gasping for breath on to the tarseal, there was only silence and a faint hint of two stroke oil in the air. “Two-strokes, these are the good guys!”

Heather hunting

She started up the gorge running until she couldn’t run any more, then walking as fast as possible until she could run again. Walk, run, walk, run. Over and over until she was like a zombie. There were tears in her eyes and a feeling of absolute desolation. Alone on foot knowing she had to get somewhere but also knowing that the chances were that there would be no one there, wherever it was, when she arrived. The tears flooding her eyes blurred and distorted reality so much it hardly mattered that it was dark... she couldn’t see anyway and she stumbled from one side of the roadway to the other almost bouncing off the barely visible changes in light at each edge of the road. She looked like a slowing pinball almost at the bottom of a pinball game. Within her was a bottomless pit as black as the night and from it came a voice that said: “It’s too late, it’s no good; they’ve gone. You’ll never see them again.” But she kept going refusing, unable to accept that she had missed what she knew was her one last chance.

It was hours later when she got home and she started right away packing up and loading her road bike. It was a single cylinder BMW with a big tank and semi-off road tyres. She topped the tank up with the spare two-stroke gas for her lawnmower. “Bit of top cylinder lubricant won’t do any harm and who cares about the catalytic converter now!”

Heather was in her late thirties, about five foot eleven, slim and good looking in a country sort of way. You had to be tough and self-reliant to look after a farm. The hours are long and the stock don’t care how you look, so country gals don’t bother with make up. Hard work and good farm eating take care of a healthy glow and a tidy body in the best possible way.

With all her warmest clothing on and her pack and bow on her back she set off to chase everyone down. Several hours later it was early in the morning and there was a hint of dawn in the eastern sky when she began to realise that they had probably stopped to camp and she had passed them without knowing it. By now she was really tired and having trouble focusing her eyes so she drove off the road, leaned the Beemer against a tree and laid down beside it on a soft bed of pine needles.

Almost immediately she was fast asleep.

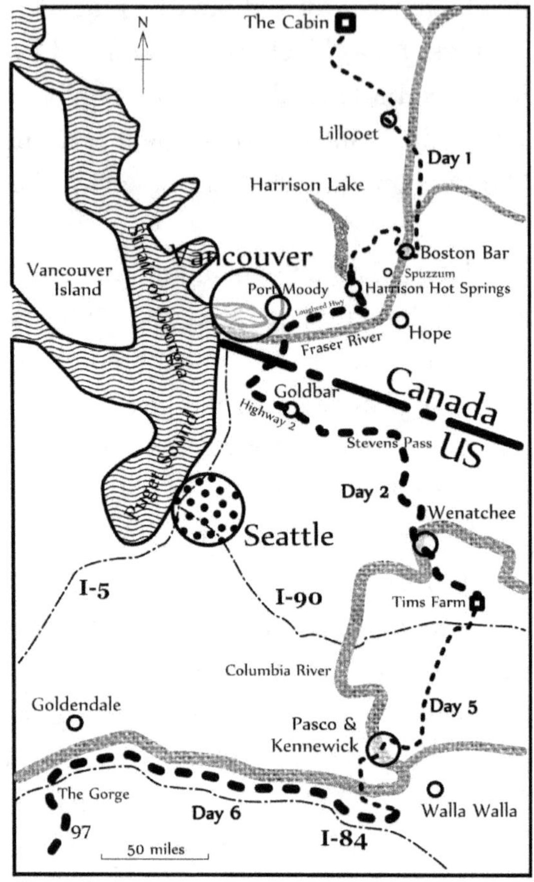

Day 6

Chapter 7, The Boneman.

Mike was the first awake and stoked up the fire to make a pot of coffee. They stood around warming themselves until the coffee was finished, then they were back on the road riding one-handed with the other held against the engine to try and keep it warm. It's pretty tricky riding with your left hand on the throttle while your right hand warms up, but you get the hang of reversing your arm movements to keep the bike in balance and the speed right... as long as you take the time to think about it. There was no traffic coming in the other direction, of course, so it really was a piece of cake. It was a beautiful morning on the plateau and the sun was just starting to come up through the rather sparse fir trees on the left of the road.

Dawn on the plateau

Underneath the tree deep in her sleep Heather dreamed she was running after someone, running and running but the more she ran the farther away they got even though they were just walking, and no matter how hard she tried she couldn't call out for them to wait. Then the people she was chasing were on motorbikes sweeping past her and had gone and faded into the distance, when she woke up, sat up and realised it was for *real*! All the motorcycles had just passed her while she slept! In the cool morning air she could hear their sound disappearing into the distance, getting fainter all the time.

She stumbled to her feet and was putting on her helmet, fumbling unsuccessfully with her cold fingers trying to latch the strap when, as if by magic, the bikes came back like a swarm of honey bees and parked all around her! Heather took her crash hat off, dropped it on the pine needles and there were tears streaming down her cheeks. A whole bunch of introductions and smiling and hugging was concluded by a small fire and a cup of tea as the sun came fully up over the horizon.

Marie smiled at Heather. "I saw your bike out of the corner of my eye. Took me awhile to overtake everyone and get them to come back."

Heather looked around at everyone. "It's so good to see friendly faces again. I've been living alone not daring to try and get to my friends in Portland. There's bad stuff happening there."

"It's bad everywhere," said Jeff. "You're coming with us, right?"

"You bet," replied Heather then she paused. "Where are you all going?"

After filling Heather in on the plan they headed off on the road spending a bit of time at Klamath Falls looking for gas, but without any luck. They figured they had about 400 miles worth

Mt. Shasta from the north

of gas for everyone and that meant they were going to make it some place the other side of Weed on I-5. Maybe as far as Redding but probably not.

After they had been back on the road for awhile they could see Mt. Shasta in the distance dominating the countryside. It was snow-topped and continuously changing with clouds forming, disappearing and then reforming, getting closer all the time. It was an absolutely beautiful sight but they all had more urgent problems on their mind.

Sparse small fir trees

Dale ran out of gas first. They were out in the middle of nowhere amongst a setting of sparse small fir trees, long dry grass and scrubby tough looking bushes. They drained some of PJ's gas first figuring he was the most frugal and then a smaller amount from everyone else. Then it was Tim who ran dry and then Dale again. By now everyone was so hyper they were slowing to 20 mph on some of the hills. This was not a fun time for anyone and their faces showed the strain every time they had to stop. They made it to I-5 and everyone waited on the freeway while just PJ and Jeff went looking for gas in Weed. There was nothing there so everyone started up and headed on south. They were driving on the left side of I-5 because it was more free of wrecks. To get off the highway for a break they made their way up the on-ramp just as they got to the town of Mount Shasta on the southern slopes of the mountain. There was an open grassy area right next door to the highway where they stopped for a brew up and a bite to eat.

The open grassy area by I-5 with Mt Shasta on the right

"It's nice not having to worry about traffic cops now," said PJ. "It used to be so annoying driving on the superslabs anywhere near heavily populated areas. People drove like robots: without any mind or thought, and the speed limits recognised that and micromanaged everything, slowing us down for every curve or big hill, leaving us with no room to use our own judgement, bombarding us with subtle, huh! hints like: 'Tired? Rest Area in 10 miles'. I mean: way to go Joe. Let's suggest to the idiots they're tired and start them falling asleep at the wheel." He paused slightly. "People regarded driving cars like they were in horizontal elevators."

Not everyone was listening to him, some were lost in their own thoughts thinking about what life had been like, and all the friends and people they had known who were now gone for ever. The accomplishments and baggage they had grown up with, the plans they had made and all the important things they had expected to do with their lives.

PJ continued:

"Ding ding. Close the door.

Ding ding. Seatbelts on.

Ding ding. Here is your death.

Ding."

"Your full of fun today PJ," said Dale. He turned to Heather.

"How do you like your Beemer?"

"It's a good road bike, too heavy for the dirt though."

"I hate four strokes with a passion," interjected PJ. "Expensive, heavy, complicated, noisy, underpowered weaklings."

"Don't hold back!" drawled Tim.

"Wave of the future!" stated Dale.

PJ grinned. "Yeah well the future didn't last long, eh! Two strokes are great. Take these Yamahas... separate oil tanks, no mixing when you fill up. Brilliant!"

"Good luck filling up!" added Mike.

PJ looked at the fire and took a sip of tea. "Actually Tim, that little XT250 you gave me is the first four stroke I've ever liked; the engine has very little braking when you wind it off, it's fairly quiet, got great disk brakes, gets really good mileage, and I can put my feet down on both sides. Brilliant!"

"Finally, enlightenment!" said Dale. "You always were pretty good at putting your feet down!" Everyone laughed!

Heather took a sip of coffee. "My dad used to ride Trials when I was a kid. It was good fun. Camping and all that. He had a 348 Montesa. Everyone brought their families and camped for the weekend. I used to help score and then my Dad bought me a small Yamaha Trials bike, a TY175. I had a load of fun on it. We had several clubs in Oregon then. There were some good old-timers too, what did they call themselves? Team Geezer—that was it! We used to get to sit round the campfire in the evening and spend the weekend at some great places; peoples farms, the forests down by Tillamook and up on the slopes of Mt. Hood and over in Washington at Bridge of the Gods. I sold my Trials bike when I got married and moved to the farm," she paused. "Before I married there was a boy I was keen on, he rode Trials and played the guitar and sang; even the blues harmonica, just like Dylan. It didn't work out. He was happy busking downtown for small change. We would both ride Trials and party on the weekend. His name was Bob," she laughed, "just like Dylan. Reckoned he was going to get his songs published and maybe be famous one day. I was in love with him but he wanted me to move in. I don't know why I didn't, I regret that now. Then everything changed when my future husband came along, and he had a farm."

"What happened to your husband?" asked Dale.

"He's dead. He had an accident on a tractor some years back."

"Sorry." Dale looked back at the fire. "I was married once but she was into weight lifting. The whole fitness thing. It didn't work out."

"We're all going to be into fitness pretty soon," said PJ.

"How far do we have to go from here?" asked Mike.

"Oh I dunno, about a thousand miles, I guess. We're going to have strong legs by the time we get there!"

"How come you use miles?" asked Dale. "I thought all you Canucks used metric."

"I grew up in Imperial and I'm dumb enough to think it's better," answered PJ with a hint of a growl in his voice. "It fits our human world. When you're dealing with people, feet and inches are perfect. You're using easy to visualise numbers: five and a half, six, six foot three. Why on earth would we measure ourselves in something as big as a yard? You'd be dealing with numbers like one point seven zero seven and one point nine zero five. Can you see the difference of the people behind those complex numbers in your mind? Me neither. You want to know how big a foot is? Look down. You're truckin' on two of them!"

"Speaking of metric," said Jeff, "I wonder what happened to Europe?"

"Maybe they changed back to Imperial seeing as how they're having to walk on foot everywhere!" drawled Tim.

"Well, they're going to have trouble walking from Paris to Dakar," said PJ. "They're going to have to swim across the straight of Gibraltar. Could be tricky. Mind you I wouldn't want to be walking in North Africa anyway. That place is full of mines left over from World War Two."

"Yeah you'd want to stick with the main roads," agreed Jeff.

PJ took a mouthful of tea and reminisced: "When we travelled across the Sahara back in the late 60s, we stopped in a small village in Algeria. I went the other side of a roll of barbed wire stretched out along the road at the edge of an empty field. I wanted to take a photo of our car through the barbed wire. We don't have military style barbed wire in New Zealand. It was just like... Wow, we're not in Kansas any more! We found out later the barbed wire was there to keep people out because the field was mined!"

"Oops!" said Kacie.

"It was on the edge of a village, actually it was *inside* the village. You'd think they'd take time out to get rid of the mines! Oh well..."

"Are there any more cookies left?" asked Tim.

"We're all out," answered Marie.

"Bummer."

"Oh what I wouldn't give for a ginger ale float right now," said Wendy.

"Make mine a cold beer," said Dale.

"Don't do this guys," said PJ. "We must concentrate on food, real food."

"No harm in dreaming," said Marie.

"Well there is actually," replied PJ. "Our bodies will adapt in time to a basic diet but it will be easier if we set our minds to it now. Imagine that: we used to eat food that was specially calorie reduced. What a bunch of idiots! I mean, we work our butts off so we can buy prepared food because we are too tired to cook and that food has to be low calorie because we don't have time, or are too lazy to get exercise."

"And then we die," added Jeff.

"Not until the giant pharmaceuticals have taken their cut," said Tim.

"Yeah, and the doctors and hospitals," said Marie.

"I reckon we were only engineered to live to about 25," stated PJ, "and we were hard-wired to eat everything we found in front of us. So here we are at 80, fat and lying in bed, kept alive by an insurance policy we worked all our life for. About the only thing we can do is prop up the bed with the electric control, so we can watch the commercials on Speed. Now, don't get me talking about NASCAR."

"Hey," said Dale. "I have some good friends racing NASCAR!"

"Good old guys," said PJ. "Speed channel used to run the world rally championship. Man those onboard shots were great. Scary as hell! I would have bought a Subaru in a flash if I'd had the dough back in those days!"

"I liked Formula 1," said Jeff, "Those three guys doing the presentation were really good."

"Yeah," said PJ, "They had a good rapport. I enjoyed listening to them."

"Supercross and Motocross were pretty good," said Tim. "Speed did them great but you're right, the world rally championships were outstanding."

"About that ginger ale float," said Kacie, "my body is crying out for a diet Coke right now!"

"Oh no!" exclaimed PJ.

"Even so," added Kacie, "I know that when you're thirsty, really thirsty, water from a cool mountain stream is like the nectar of the Gods."

"I predict that cool mountain streams and lush green valleys are in our future." said PJ with a grin. "Of course we don't know where we're going right now and we don't really have a clue what will be there when we get there." He paused. "We don't even know where 'there' is. It's all unknown, but the great thing about the future is... anything can happen, any wonderful-good thing."

"That picture of cool mountain streams and green valleys is something we should cling to," said Kacie.

"But there's some wastelands and deserts to cross before we get there," added PJ, "there's always waste lands and desert."

They continued to sit around the fire talking quietly. No one was keen to go back on the road and get to the point where they had to ditch the bikes.

"Who are you?" The voice came from somewhere behind some bushes on the edge of the field they were in. "Are you Wiremen?" They couldn't see anyone.

"What the hell is a Wireman?" asked Tim.

"You string wire across the road and kills people."

“Hell no,” said Jeff. “We’re just passing through.”

“Passing through. On I-5? You crazy, you head’n straight for the Wiremen. They kills you for sure.”

There was a long pause and a man in his early 50’s walked out into the open. He carried a hunting bow and had a large knife in a pouch on his waist. He looked pretty good on his feet, and sharp with it.

“Name’s Napoleon, friends call me the Boneman.” He grinned and put his bow down. They introduced themselves and gave him a mug of coffee.

“How do you spell your name?” said the Boneman to Kacie.

“K-a-c-i-e, but you pronounce it KC, it’s an old Irish name.”

“How come you use a bow?” asked Dale.

“It don’t make no noise, and I gets to eat all my kill, myself.”

“Otherwise who gets it?” asked Jeff.

“You use a gun in these parts, the Wiremen come lookin’ for you, then they gets your kill; and maybe they gets you.”

“Seems reasonable!” said Dale.

“Only people who use guns round here is Wiremen,” said the Boneman. “You hears a gun you gets the hell out y’hear me, fast as you can,” he paused. “Where you guys headen?”

“Mexico,” answered Jeff.

“Hmm. Mexico huh, never been to Mexico; pretty warm there ain’t it?”

“That’s the plan,” said Tim. “These four started off in British Columbia, and we all came along for the ride. My daughter Wendy, Marie and her daughter Sandy and me, are from Washington. Dale and Heather here are from Oregon. We figure Mexico would be a smart place to be this winter. We figure it’s going to get too cold to live up in these parts.” The town of Mt. Shasta was up at about 6000 feet and it was cold out in the open. The mountain itself to the north of them was an extinct volcano about 14,000 ft high.

There was another pause. The Boneman was looking around at them and their bikes. He was clearly going through a sea-change in his mind. His eyes opened a bit wider and he half smiled: "Ya got room for one more?"

"Well yeah," said PJ. "But we're just about out of gas. We're gonna be walking in twenty, maybe forty miles."

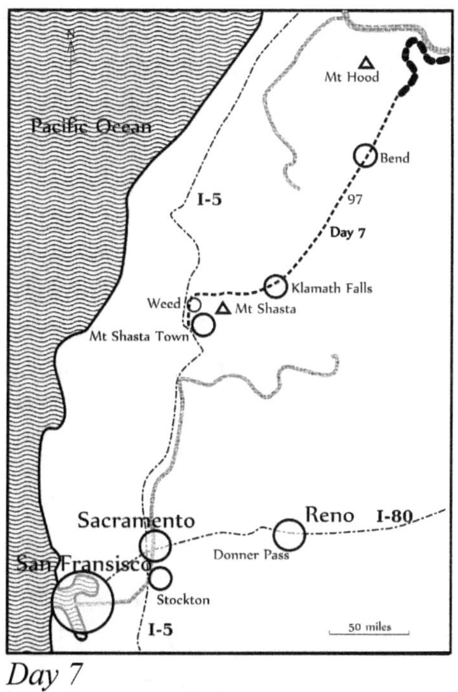

Day 7

"No problem!" said the Boneman. Turned out he had a stash of gas at his house a few miles away.

"Talk about luck," said Dale.

The Boneman "borrowed" one of his neighbour's trail bikes.

"Don't know where my neighbours are but I figure they ain't comin' back for this." He grinned. "Guess it's too bad anyway!"

"These Wiremen are only on I-5?" asked Jeff.

"Yep. Far's I know. They's down by where it narrows near Shasta Lake. You can't get by them, no-how."

"We can take a jog across and through to Reno a few miles south of here," said PJ. "I've been that way a couple of times when I was competing at Donner. Smaller road but no problem."

"Yeah, I know where you mean," said the Boneman. "That road's OK. The coast road, 101, got dumped into the sea with the quakes. But what we gonna do for gas, I mean we gonna get half way to LA, that's all," he paused. "I got a gal I used to date near Bakersfield. She might have some, but we ain't gonna get that far."

"Y'know," said Jeff, "we might be able to get gas with some of the California Trials guys. Dale you know where Andy and June live, they run their business out of their home don't they? I think they were up against the mountains near Sacramento."

"I know where June and Andy live," said Tim, "stopped by for some parts once. Hell, guess it's worth a try."

It took all the next day to get the Boneman set up on his "borrowed" trail bike, so they spent a second night at his house. (It was getting to be a really good atmosphere amongst them, almost like they were an extended family unit. Everyone had gelled and there was no bickering or shouting)—except when someone played a practical joke on someone else!

The next morning they followed the Boneman out on a back road. He wanted to check out the junction off of I-5 that they had to take to bypass the Wiremen's territory that was further south on the interstate. It was barely light as they parked the bikes and the Boneman and most of the guys walked around a long curve in the road to look at the junction. As they walked cautiously along following him he stopped suddenly and motioned them to get to the side of the road. They all crept forward to peer around the rest of the bend. The Wiremen had set up a road block on highway 89. They had a couple of pickups parked blocking the highway just where it came off I-5.

"Just as well we checked," said Tim quietly.

"They must be blocking this because it's the only other way south apart from I-5," said the Boneman.

Dale stretched his head up to get a good look. "I think there's only two of them."

Jeff was cautiously looking over the Boneman's shoulder. "Is there another way for us to get past?"

"Yeah, I reckon," answered the Boneman. "But they'll hear us where we rejoin the road. We can cut across out the back on Old McCloud road and take several fire roads and tracks through the forest. We rejoin half way up the cutting about a mile away. We may have to do some bushwhacking, 'cos there's probably some deadfall." He paused. "It's pretty rough in places. I think I'm gonna have trouble getting my bike through."

"We can get your bike through," said Jeff.

"You're probably going to have to help me too," added Heather. "The Beemer is way too heavy for me to go very far off road."

One of the Wiremen got out of the pickup to take a leak and as he walked to the side of the road they could plainly hear one of his boots squeaking with every step. "I had a pair of boots like that once," said Dale. "Drove me crazy. Gave them to a homeless guy in Portland."

"These homeless guys get around don't they!" drawled Tim.

Dale took a closer look at the checkpoint through his binoculars. "They've only got two pickups. Reckon if I take out their tyres they won't be able to chase us and the pickups will block the road. Well, maybe they'll block the road. I might be able to hole their gas tanks too, that'll slow them down!"

"Can you do all that fast?" asked the Boneman. "You're not that far away and they could rush you."

Dale patted his thirty-ought six. "You bet! This baby will take down a mountain goat at 2000 ft. I can take out two pickups at 400, no problem. Let them rush me and they're dead meat!"

"Hmm, OK," said PJ. "Well we better get everyone up the track as far as possible without them hearing us before you start taking pot shots at them! Dale you better come too and leave your heavy stuff up with us. Then you can make a fast run back when you're done taking their vehicles out."

The Boneman pointed up the dirt bank at the side of the road. "Dale, you be better off up in the bushes, that way they won't be able to spot you. You gonna take them out too?"

"No," replied Dale, "there's no need, they'll never catch us on foot..."

Chapter 8, The Wiremen.

They backtracked down the road to where they had parked the bikes and then the Boneman led them off into the trees and vegetation to where Dale could get a clear shot at the pickups. The last few yards they had to fight their way through the tough scrubby bushes before they could see the junction.

The junction seen from the bushes

Dale looked around. “I’ll have to take the shots kneeling, there’s nowhere to lie down.”

“Will that be a problem?” asked PJ.

“No. Better. I can change targets faster.”

They walked back to the bikes. Tim turned to the Boneman. “How far past the junction will we get back to the road?”

“About three quarters of a mile, maybe a mile. They’ll head to where the shots are coming from anyway. Take them a while to figure out which way we’re going.”

“Is there any way you can get their vehicles to catch on fire?” asked Wendy.

“Not unless they’re dumb enough to be smoking near the

gas," replied Dale.

The Boneman grinned. "They dumb enough!"

"Betcha life they'll get some other wheels and hunt us down," said Tim.

"Guess we don't have a choice," figured Jeff. "Jeez, it's gonna be Mad Max, *for real*, and they've got more guns. We better plan on riding all night unless we come across some place they can't get their four wheelers through."

"How far is it to where you guys will wait?" asked Dale.

"About three, maybe four miles," said the Boneman.

"Hey, you bastards better wait for me!" Dale was only half joking, but everyone laughed.

PJ thought about it. "Actually we'd be best to leave you here Dale. I'll go with these guys to make sure I know the way. Then I'll come back for you and when I get here you can take those pickups out." He turned to the others. "When you guys hear the shots you get to the road and ride down it as long as it takes for Dale and me to catch up. Don't wait for us, keep an eye out behind you, don't crash, and *don't race*. You have to take the turn off on to 44 and then 395 to get to Reno. You got that?" They all nodded.

"44 and then 395," said Mike. PJ paused and looked down at the ground. He looked back up. "If something comes up behind you with four wheels... Then go like hell, because you're on you're own." There was silence as everyone tried not to think about that possibility. "I'll give you my maps." PJ got the clear plastic bag containing his maps out of his pack and gave it to Tim.

"Come on, we got to get moving," said the Boneman. "PJ, you goin' to have any trouble finding your way back?"

"Mm, mm. No problem." PJ was very confident of his ability to find his way and prided himself on his memory for roads and places he had been to. Jeff did not have anywhere near as high a confidence of PJ's guiding ability as PJ had of himself, but Jeff's own sense of direction was real bad so he didn't say anything.

Everyone started their bikes up and disappeared up the road while Dale got his hunting gear out and began to walk back through the brush.

The forest track off Old McCloud road

The forest track off of Old McCloud road was really quite easy but there were a couple of places where trees had fallen across and the Boneman and Heather had to have their bikes ridden for them through the brush to get around the trees. Marie and Sandy needed a couple of people pushing them at these places too.

There was one place where a stream had washed the track away and everyone needed help to get across. Next they turned off the main track and headed right, then left about a quarter of a mile later at another junction.

The forestry track was really quite easy to begin with

The track was now barely more than a walking trail and very rough in places. The Boneman low-sided off his bike on the last downhill but picked himself up and carried on. He hadn't got the idea yet that you had to aim for the low parts of the ruts on the track... because that was where the wheels were going to go anyway.

In sight of 89

When they had almost got to 89 everyone stopped and shut their bikes down while they were still behind the trees and shrubs out of sight of the road. While PJ rode back to Dale, the Boneman and Tim walked on down to the road to check it out. It was empty and had an innocent air about it, quiet, with no hint of danger.

Dale was sitting down and looking through his binoculars when PJ arrived back. He turned to PJ and handed him the binoculars. "You hang on to these. We're going to have to move fast." He got onto his knees, loaded the first round, and put the rifle up to his shoulder.

The road was empty and had an innocent air about it...

The Wiremen had had another night of nothing to do and were bored and tired and ready for their replacements to arrive so they could go eat and sleep. They woke up in a hurry as the first bullet hit the front left tyre with the almost simultaneous crack from the rifle. Thwack. Bang. "Geesus Kee-ryst what the hell is going on!" yelled one of them as the pickup slumped down on the flat tyre. The guy in the passenger seat opened the passenger door and bolted while the driver clambered across the centre console and was almost out of the door when the second shot took out the rear tyre. They were both heading for cover as the gas tank took a direct hit. One of them had ditched his smoke in his hurry to get to safety and the cigarette was directly in the path of the stream of gasoline pouring out of the vehicle on to the warm road surface! They were still running when Dale took out the tyres of their other pickup and at that point the gasoline reached the cigarette by the first vehicle and burst into flames.

The Wiremen had changed their direction and were running to the other vehicle to grab some weapons from it as Dale pumped another shot, holing the gas tank of the second vehicle. Now the other Wireman dropped his smoke in fright and the second pickup went up in flames. At this point they figured they were under full scale attack and they both dived for cover into the ditch on the edge of the road! Dale and PJ were turning to go back to their bikes when everything turned on its head... the Wiremen's day shift arrived. "Godammit," said Dale. "There's another pickup. And no clear shot. Let's get the hell out of here, we can't afford to get into a firefight, there's too many of them."

"Let's go!" replied PJ.

They scrambled back to the bikes, Dale loaded up, and they got the hell out of there. PJ led Dale through the town to Old McCloud road and then off on to the fire road. There they did their best to motocross their wallowing overladen bikes, riding with an urgency they had not had before. But when they got to where PJ had left the others, they could see the Wiremen's replacement pickup had beaten them to it! They saw the pickup through the trees as it flashed past them up the highway. It was full of people and chasing hell bent after the other bikes, leaving a haze of oil smoke behind it. The two of them stopped as they got to the tarseal and looked up the road in disbelief.

"They must have figured out what the hell we were up to," said PJ. "They're smarter than we thought!"

"Damn, we gotta get after them," said Dale. So the two of them got on the gas and went flat out after the pickup.

The others were waiting for about a half hour before they heard the first shot. Then as the other shots followed they all rode carefully down to 89 and started off up the road. The Boneman was out in front as he was the slowest and Tim was at the rear keeping an eye out behind for PJ and Dale. They figured it would take them about an hour to catch up to the group even though they were the two fastest riders.

89 was a single lane road winding about and following the contours of the hills. They passed through a small town and then about fifteen miles later they were starting to relax when Tim saw the pickup about two miles behind them. His head snapped round and he sped up shouting to everyone to gas it as he passed them.

89 – straight as an arrow through a fish-eye lens

They were on a really long straight stretch of road that now appeared even longer. It went on and on dead straight with the pickup getting ever closer.

The wide right hand corner

Finally, after what seemed like forever, there was a wide right hand corner and as they got round it they saw two large firs had fallen and were completely blocking the road. Tim didn't hesitate and charged off the road through the light brush and around the upended roots of the downed trees, but the Boneman stopped unsure of what to do. Everyone else gassed it and rode their bikes following in Tim's tyre tracks. Heather had to get off and push her big Beemer but got it through without help. The Boneman then tried to follow Heather but took it too slow and he fell off sideways in the loose soft dirt and pine-needles, getting his leg trapped under the side of the bike.

The fallen trees

Tim and Mike went back to help the Boneman, shouting and waving to the girls to keep going down the road. They lifted the bike off the Bonemans leg and were struggling to push the bike around the roots of the trees together with the Boneman... when the Wiremen's truck came barrelling round the corner. All hell broke loose as the truck slid to a halt with six guys jumping out and opening fire at them. The girls (who hadn't kept going) and Jeff ran back and kneeled down behind the fallen trees. There they let loose a volley of arrows, nailing one of the Wiremen who was standing out in the open with a 9mil machine gun. The others had a miscellaneous collection of assault rifles and hand guns and were using the pickup for cover. Marie and Sandy were pumping shot after shot at the Wiremen from their rifles and the sound of the girls bullets slamming and zinging off the metal were helping to make the Wiremen's own firing very ineffectual. Just then PJ and Dale rounded the corner and rode their bikes flat out into the trees on the side of the road. They dumped their bikes on the ground and using the trees for cover ran closer to the action. The Wiremen were now surrounded. PJ took out one of them putting an arrow into his side while Dale let rip with his thirty-ought six and took out another one of them. Dale's rifle shot from behind them had the Wiremen's attention and one got downed by Kacie as they headed for cover into the trees.

Meanwhile, Tim and Mike had the Boneman's bike back close to the road and Tim rode it off to where the girls bikes were parked while Mike took off running to get his bow. The Boneman loaded an arrow, aimed, and with a following shot took out one of the Wiremen running through the trees. While all this was going on the pickup driver was trying to turn around in the road when Dale took him out with a head shot and the pickup ran into the ditch and stalled.

Now Heather ran down the edge of the road after the last of the Wiremen as he escaped through the trees. But he saw her coming for him and took off deeper into the forest. Heather followed fully taken up by the heat of battle and soon she was scrambling down a steep incline. A few seconds later she realised... that she wasn't following anyone any more. Her eyes opened up wide as she stopped and listened... there was silence in the forest, no sound. "He must be hiding," she thought to herself, "But where, ahead or behind?" She looked all round her but saw and heard nothing. Just then her feet slipped and her legs became trapped in a deep hole that had been covered in leaves and bark-mulch; it was the remains of where an uprooted tree had once grown. As she tried to pull her legs out, she heard something coming down the hill behind her. A rustling, crunching and sliding sound, and then there was silence again. She stopped trying to free her legs and listened motionless. The noise started up again but now plainly it was footsteps. Heavy footsteps heading her way... and one boot had a squeak. Crunch squeak, crunch squeak; closer and closer.

Back on the road there was silence as everyone stood still and looked in shock through the dust in the air at the dead lying all around them. The silence seemed to last forever.

Eventually PJ spoke: "Is anyone hit? Girls are you all right?"

The women looked at each other. "We're fine, no ones hurt," said Marie. She paused. "Where's Heather?"

Everyone looked around at everyone else and then PJ said. "Where's Jeff?" Then loudly: "Heather, Jeff where are you?"

Back in the forest the footsteps were almost on top of Heather and as she looked up she saw this mountain of a man towering over her. When he saw her his face lit up and he let out a roar of vindication, triumph and revenge. He reached to the pouch on his waist and whipped out a big hunting knife. He stared balefully down at her with a nasty smile showing two rows of uncared for tobacco-stained teeth. Then he flipped the knife into the air and caught it again, savouring the moment. Heather screamed as he lunged at her with the knife and *at that instant* an arrow pierced the wireman's back. The knife dropped from his hand and for a brief moment his eyes looked down at the bloody head of the arrow sticking out of his chest. He moved his hands to grasp the shaft of the arrow, then with an inarticulate choking-gurgling sound, frothy blood oozed and trickled from his mouth and he tumbled away down the hill, dead.

Jeff came rushing down to Heather. "Are you all right?" Heather nodded, too overcome by emotion to speak. Jeff reached under her arms from behind her and helped pull her legs free of the hole and as her legs came free the two of them collapsed back on to the dirt bank. Recovering, Heather partially turned her head to him and said softly, "that was pretty good timing!" Then Jeff noticed he was holding his arms around her under her breasts. Embarrassed, he let her go. A tiny sigh escaped Heather's mouth. "Can you walk?" he asked, standing up. "Yes," said Heather and she held her hand up for him to grasp. As she did this she smiled at him in the way only a woman can smile at a man. As he pulled her up she said quietly to him: "Your arms felt so good around me!" and she stumbled not quite by accident forward into his arms again...

Back on the road everyone was starting to get frantic, when Heather and Jeff walked out of the forest together holding hands.

There was a stunned silence, then Tim drawled "What have you guys been doing in the bush? Don't you know there's some fighting going on!"

Heather and Jeff collapsed into each others arms with nervous laughter and everyone smiled as Dale pushed Tim on the shoulder and said, "geez, don't embarrass the poor kids!"

Sandy was shaking, so Marie held her close and said very quietly like she was a small child again, "it's OK, it's all OK, we're going to be fine. It's all right now."

PJ and Dale picked up their bikes and rode them through the forest past the fallen trees. Then everyone got together to talk out what had happened. The Boneman and Tim straightened out the damage on his bike and the rest of them siphoned the Wire-men's pickup of gas and topped up all their tanks.

Finally everyone got back on their bikes and the now decidedly jittery convoy headed off on their journey south once again.

Chapter 9, Trapped!

The spectacular view from the rest area

They spent the night off the highway in a rest area with a spectacular view, where they could see the road they had just come along below them in the bottom of the valley. While the girls prepared a meal the others took turns watching the road just in case anyone else was following them. There was a small herd of deer grazing about a hundred yards away so Mike and Jeff stalked and shot one of them with their bows. Later, as the day turned into evening, the quietness of the forest coupled with the smell of wood smoke and roasting deer was like a healing ointment on a wound—and they felt the danger and tension of the day beginning to ease away.

When it was time to eat, Marie's daughter Sandy was sitting like a stone at the picnic table, just staring at her food and not touching it. "What's up," asked Mike. "Is something wrong?"

"She's a vegetarian," explained Marie.

PJ took a deep breath. "Oh boy, mmkay. Sandy, we don't have the luxury of choosing our food any more," he leaned towards her and touched her gently on the shoulder. "I know it's easy for me to say this, but you have to change. If you don't eat what we kill, you will get weaker and weaker until eventually we all have to stop somewhere and watch you die." He took another deep breath. "I'm not exaggerating, we don't have a choice, we have to eat everything. This isn't a game, no one is going to rescue us if we get lost, there's no chopper waiting to lift us out, no farmers markets with swathes of delicious healthy vegetables and fruits, no supermarkets with lots of good organic stuff, no restaurants featuring organic pasta or special 'healthy' dishes on their menu. There's no menus any more. Hey," PJ shook her gently on the shoulder, "we're going to survive and we want you coming with us. Don't make us bury you young." He paused to let his words sink in. "Why don't you try a small bit that's been well done," he stood up. "Here I'll get you a piece." He took her plate and removed the meat that was still partially red, replacing it with a really tasty well done piece and handed it back to her. Then he looked around at everyone else and motioned for them to *stop staring at her.* "Just take a small bite and chew it well, then swallow."

Sandy braced herself. "OK, I'll give it a try." She cut a small piece off, put it in her mouth and chewed with no expression on her face. She chewed some more, paused and swallowed. In spite of PJ's cautioning look everyone was frozen in place, their eyes locked on Sandy. They didn't have long to wait. Without any warning she leapt to her feet, ran towards the trees as though she was drunk, doubled over and threw up violently. She crouched there, her shoulders heaving every time some new portion of food came up. Slowly the convulsions died away and a few minutes later she came back and sat down. Jeff handed her a tissue. "I think I'll be all right now," she said.

It was a lovely place to camp, high up and overlooking a continuous stretch of forest as far as they could see—all the way to the mountains and hills on the horizon. It would be nicer though if they didn't still have the feeling of being hunted.

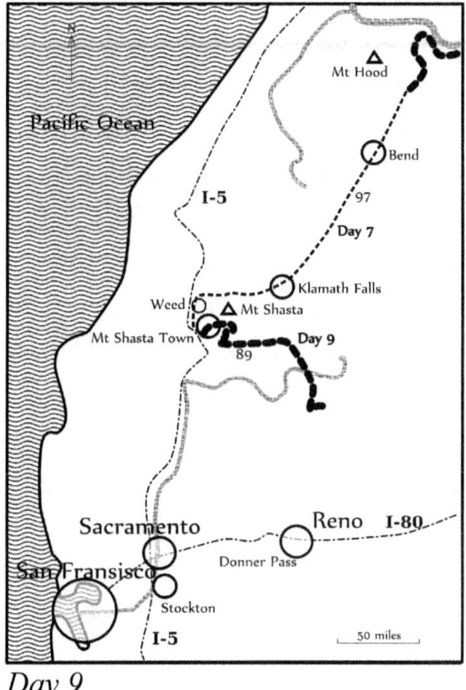

Day 9

Early the next morning the forest was especially beautiful with patches of gold and amber amongst the dark green of the firs. The forest already knew there was a long winter coming.

The inland plain before Reno

It was a long hot drive over a series of inland plains before they got to Reno. Somewhere on these plains there was a large jetliner that had crashed. The tail section had ripped off and was upside-down followed by the broken off middle sticking up in the air with the cockpit nose down ploughed into the ground. They could see the gouge marks across the fields as it had tried to land. It looked like someone was still alive and waving at them to come and help, but as they approached they could see it was just a bright red jacket caught up in a bush with one arm loose and flapping around in the wind. When they got to the fuselage they didn't stay, all that was left was the remains of bodies and other debris scattered around. Not a good place to be.

Reno was a real mess but they got through the city OK after a bit of off-road riding to bypass the wrecks on the highways. They hung a right on the superslab and headed west towards Truckee. On the way they found a huge camping and outdoor store right alongside the main highway. The store had been looted but there were still a few hunting bows including a real high-tech one that Dale took a liking to. It had wheels and some sort of compound frame. Marie and Sandy exchanged their rifles for bows and they all loaded up on arrows and knives and spare strings. There were some packs, too. Nice ones. They were hidden under a huge store exhibit of stuffed animals on a mountainside of wood, plastic and paper mache. The whole thing had collapsed and buried the packs.

"Y'know something," said Tim, "these packs are top of the line. Way better than the ones we've got. Damn this is a great find!"

Jeff stuck his head out of the fitting rooms. "Hey guys, take a look at this." Inside on the floor there was a big pile of some really tough, thick outdoor clothing that someone had been trying on. The material was so thick it was just like canvas.

"This stuff will last forever!" said PJ. No big sizes though, but Heather, Wendy, and PJ picked out great combinations each of long thick khaki coloured pants with extra pockets down the side and tough bush jackets, long-sleeved shirts, hats and hiking boots.

"This is good walking stuff," Wendy said. "We're going to need this."

Tim found a really nice pocket compass tucked away in a drawer and gave it to PJ.

"Brilliant," said PJ. "You can have my old one, it's not as fancy as this but it will do in an emergency. I bought it to align my satellite dish at home but it's good enough to help you trekking through the woods and it seems tough enough. We're going to need compasses in a few years when the roads start to disappear."

They reached Truckee by late afternoon but found the interstate was blocked to the west of the town with a huge rock slide so they went back and turned onto the old Donner road. They decided they would spend the night at the ski lodge at the top of the pass. This was where many big Trials events had been held in the past and it would almost feel like home.

PJ motioned for them to stop at the park on the lakeside just off the interstate. "I'm going to spend a bit of time here by myself and visit a chalet just up the road. This was where I had my last date back in the early 80's at a world championship round. Got a lot of good memories from here." There was silence for awhile.

Wendy put her hand on his arm. "We'll wait for you up at the ski lodge,."

PJ nodded. "I may spend the night down here."

Lakeside at the foot of Donner Pass

After everyone left he walked towards the lakes edge, sat down on a log, and cried his heart out. It was late afternoon when he went to see if the chalet was still there. It was and it looked in good condition. He got off the bike and tried the door, it was unlocked. Everything inside was pretty much like he remembered it as he walked around from room to room. He went to the garage, swung open the door and pushed the bike in. He had a strange feeling as he did this, as if someone was watching him, but put it down to memories of his girlfriend. Nonetheless he locked the garage door. Out back on the patio he could see a huge blackberry tangle on the edge of the yard, loaded with fruit. Mostly black and fully ripe but looking closer as he picked and ate he could see that there were many more berries still green hiding behind the half-ripe berries that were just starting to turn red.

A Black-Headed Grosbeak flew in and picked industrially through the grass and weeds partially covering the dry dusty ground in the back yard. The tiny bird came within a few feet of him, seemingly completely unafraid. It stopped now and then to take several bites on the bigger seeds it had found, but then immediately was back to work... peck, peck, move, peck, move, peck. On and on. The Grosbeak stopped eating only once to look up at him slowly picking fruit off the bush.

That evening he warmed up some cans of food he found in a cupboard using the propane stove in the cabin. Then he went to sleep surrounded by memories on the large double bed in the master bedroom.

The top of Donner Pass looking back down at the lake.

After the others left PJ at the campground by the lake it took only a few minutes to get to the top of Donner Pass and into the parking lot of the ski lodge. There they were astounded to find June and Andy and two of their friends Jason and Samantha (Sam) holed up with the big team van and several bikes. June and Andy were the ones from the California Trials club they were going to try and get gas from! They had managed to escape from the Sacramento area along a back road and while they were at the ski lodge they had had to fight off an attack by a gang.

"We shot two of them," said June. "But they got Andy in the leg and I kind of went berserk and went after them. I got one more but then the others quit. We've been expecting them to come back and have another go." No one else from the local Trials community had turned up and they were overjoyed to see the guys from the Pacific Northwest.

June and Andy were British. Andy was a tough sturdy northern lad, a bit quiet and taciturn but a good guy to have on your side in a fight. June was bubbly and full of life, slim and a real pretty gal. Jason and Sam were in their early thirties, the same age as June and Andy. Jason was a spectacular Trials rider who earned a good living doing demo's on his Trials bike at shows all over the US. Sam was a good Trials rider too, but she was better known as a black belt Judo and kick-boxing expert who worked as a stuntwomen in movies. She had done motorcycle stunts in many of the big Hollywood movies of the last ten years.

"It's so good to see you, it's been rather scary up here for us," said June after all the hugging and introductions had stopped. "Where are you heading for, surely not here?"

"Mexico, we think Baja right now," replied Jeff.

"What are you guys going to do in Baja?" Andy said.

"Haven't you seen the ads?" drawled Tim. "We're going to lie on the beach and drink Mexican beer!" Everyone laughed!

"Well we've got a bunch of seeds PJ brought with him. He's real good with growing things," said Mike.

"PJ is with you?" asked June.

"He's stopped off for a bit of solitude to reminisce down at the bottom of the hill," replied Jeff. "We're glad he's along. He's a good gardener. We figure on growing our own food and maybe there will be some fruit trees and other local stuff."

"We have a bad feeling for winter up north," added Mike.

"Yeah," said Kacie. "We figure very few people will survive the cold if winter is as long as summer."

June was looking at them with big open eyes. "Winter in Baja sounds pretty good to me! You reckon bikes are the way to go?"

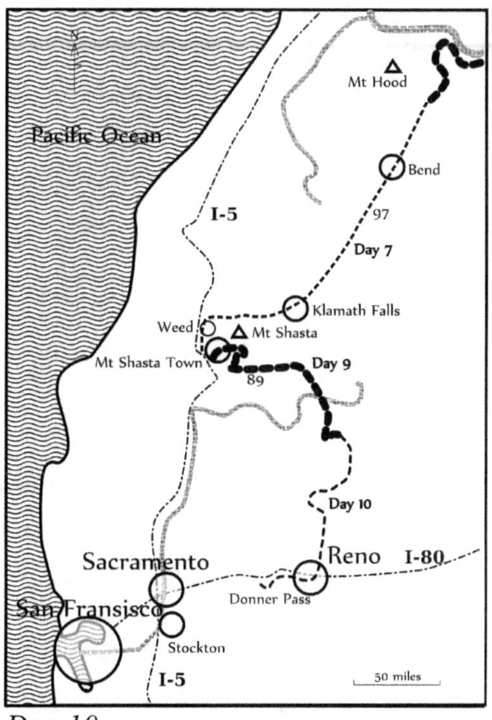

Day 10

"We wouldn't have got here on four wheels," answered Mike. "Some places are messed up real bad. There's no other way to get through except on a bike. Trees are down, abandoned vehicles, wrecks, and roadblocks mostly in the bigger towns, garbage all over the place, and bodies."

"Are the roadblocks manned?" asked Jason.

"Apparently up around Vancouver they were but we by-passed that," said Jeff. "We saw only one that was manned, up by Mt. Shasta."

"We shot our way through," said Dale.

"Yeah, they chased us," added the Boneman. "Caught us when we were held up by a couple of downed trees across the road. We wiped them out in a firefight."

June was definitely looking a bit wild eyed now.

Wendy looked at her and said, "it's them or us. It's an easy decision."

"Yeah," agreed Dale, "a no-brainer."

June nodded. She didn't trust her voice.

PJ was deep asleep down in the chalet when... *Boom.*

The sound was huge and the dull reverberations echoed through the empty house.

Boom.

He was standing up even before the second crash came and knew exactly what was happening even though it had never happened to him before; there was a gang chucking a huge rock at one of the doors to smash it in. So PJ did what everyone would have done in the circumstances—he panicked. A stream of thoughts went through his mind as he looked around. What could he do? He was trapped. There was no way out, no basement or loft to hide in, and the windows all had bars to keep people out, or in this case, in. "The bike!" he thought. "Yes, get to the bike." He ran down the corridor and past the kitchen just as the kitchen door burst down and a machete hurled past his head embedding itself in the wall. He focused on doing only what was essential and in two more steps he had reached the living room door, opened it and swung it shut behind him. As it closed, his other hand turned the key in the lock and at that instant he felt a hand turn the handle from the other side. Whoa dude, that was as close as it gets!

He went into the garage from the living room and then remembered he had left the key for the garage door with his backpack... in the bedroom. He was still trapped, but now in the living room and garage. Running through his head were the thoughts: "Not me. Not now. I'm not ready. What can I do?" Then he remembered the alarm system that was hooked up to a panic button on the living room wall. Was it still working? It had a pretty big battery. He went to it and pushed the button. Woop—Woop—Woop—Woop. The huge fire alarm up in the rafters took off and he could hear the gang panicking and running around to the front of the house. Oh wow, now he had to unlock the door and get back to the bedroom. He paused. Would they have left someone guarding the door?

Guessing not, he braced himself, unlocked the door and stepped quickly over the rubble in the corridor from the smashed down kitchen door. He grabbed his pack in the bedroom and as he ran back to the living room he could hear the gang shouting at him and breaking the windows as they came round the side of the house back to the kitchen. They had realised there was no one coming to his aid. He locked himself back in the living room and went into the garage. There he turned the bike around to face the garage door. With the bike leaning on its sidestand he turned the gas tap on, put the bike in third gear, and swung the kick start lever out. He put his pack on his back and walked to the garage door but his whole body was shaking uncontrollably, so he paused and took another deep breath. Would there be anyone outside the door? There was no way to tell. He braced himself again, then he unlocked the padlock on the garage door and quietly slid the bolts on both sides back out of the wall. The garage door was now balanced and free to swing open.

He walked back to the bike, kicked the sidestand up and got

on the bike. He pulled the clutch in and paused slightly, gathering all his senses together, and then he switched the ignition on. Without any further conscious thought he placed his foot on the kick starter, threw his body in the air, and as his body dropped gave the kickstarter a swing with every ounce of energy he had. *Instantly* the bike roared into life. He wound the throttle open, dropped the clutch and smashed the door open with the front wheel. The back wheel spun on the gravel of the driveway and as he picked up speed he clicked fourth gear and rocketed out past the front of the house where he could see the dark outline of one of the gang who had been left on guard at the front *running at him*. There was a flash of light and a sharp crack as the man fired a handgun at PJ who was really on it and drifting sideways tapped out towards him. But he misjudged the speed of the bike and missed. He fired twice more but he was partially blinded by the muzzle flash and there was nothing but darkness to aim at. PJ flew safely past him and out onto the small side road—his throttle wide open and the engine wailing. He was free!

He hadn't turned the lights on, but as he looked ahead instinctively he looked up, not down at the blackness of the invisible road. His eyes were so wide open he could tell where the road was from the tops of the trees and the lighter night sky above making a virtual mirror of the roadway down below. It was like riding upside down in the light clouds on a pathway in the stars.

He turned right and then right again a half mile or so later and followed the mountain pass up towards the ski lodge at the summit. There were very few trees on the pass so in front of him the stars lit the road with the pale grey half-light of freedom all the way, all the wonderful ice cold way to the top. But PJ felt no cold after being so close to the absolute zero of death.

It took about fifteen minutes to reach the lodge, and the soft warm feeling of being alive made the stream of frozen mountain air past his body like the touch of a lover's hand leading you finally to bed.

From this day on, he was going to know *forever* that it was so good to be alive!

Chapter 10, Donner Ski Lodge.

Back at the ski lodge everyone was sitting around in the old bar area. "Hey have you noticed how long the seasons are?" asked Jeff. "Summer was almost a year long! What the hell is going on? We're still in Autumn, this should be the height of winter."

"What are we going to do about the calendar?" asked Sam. "Is this something to do with those damn nuclear bombs? Idiots!"

"We heard one report on shortwave that a giant meteorite hit India," replied June.

"I saw it," said Heather. "It was like a giant fireball streaking across the night sky. I was out checking on the cattle. That sort of thing, stuff like partial eclipses of the sun, really upsets cattle. They know something is wrong. I could hear them lowing."

"Lowing?" asked Jeff.

"Mooing," replied Heather with a smile.

"Maybe it was the meteorite that caused those huge dust clouds in the upper atmosphere," said Mike.

"That and the fires," Dale noted. "Man, there was over a month I didn't see the sun because of the smoke."

"We're all that's left, damn near," said Mike.

"Oh there must be some places hanging in there," said Heather. "With wind power and solar panels."

"Yeah, but what are they going to do for food?" asked Kacie.

"It doesn't grow outside, not in the winter," said Jeff. "They won't be prepared. Like the original Donner party back in the 1800's, they'll starve to death." There was a silence.

"Yeah the Donner party had to cannibalise their dead to stay alive," said Andy.

"Oh some of them will make it," said Mike. "Grow food indoors or in greenhouses."

"Sprout salad anyone?" joked Dale. No one laughed. "Wonder what happened to all the nuclear subs?" he added.

"Bet half of them sent their missiles to Iran and the other half to North Korea!" said Jeff.

"Wonder what happened to Russia?" said June.

"Oh didn't you hear? The Berlin wall came down!" The voice came from a big vicious looking man walking in. He was carrying an assault rifle at the ready and behind him was a swaggering group of really nasty looking characters dressed in camouflage clothing. They were all carrying weapons: black semi-automatic 9mm hand guns, machine guns and assault rifles, and they had big hunting knives strapped to their waists. They had bandanna's or cowboy hats on their heads and heavy black commando style boots. Most of them had green and black camouflage make-up all over their faces. They looked like really bad dudes, and they knew it. There was a shocked silence as the gang fanned out into the room.

"OK," said the leader with authority. "All of you lie down on the floor and put your hands behind your back. Ziggy get the ties on them."

Ziggy was one of those who had camouflage paint on his face. He might have had some naval training because as he leered at the friends on the floor he let out a machine gun belch in which he voiced the words "Aye aye. Sir!"

The rest of the gang grinned in appreciation at his skill with his voice. Ziggy went around strapping zip ties to hold everyone's wrists together. "Shut your mouths. Don't pull any tricks and we might let you live," said the leader. He paused and smiled; it was not a nice smile. It was the sort of smile you would get out of a poisonous snake preparing to strike. "OK," he said, then very slowly savouring his words: "Now we're going to play a game." His gang chuckled and grinned in anticipation. "It's called, Gang Bang. Who's going to be first to play?"

He looked around at all the scared faces and stopped at Sam. Jason was frantic but like everyone else could do nothing but watch. The leader strolled up to Sam, pulled her to her feet then wriggled his body against hers. Then he put his arms around her and his hands on her ass and stroked it, letting his fingers ease gently between the cheeks. "Oh yes," he said slowly with great emotion. "Feel that gorgeous butt. Mmm, it's, you!"

Ziggy cut the zip tie from Sam's wrists as four of the gang grabbed her arms and legs and spread-eagled her struggling body on a table. Black belt or not, there was nothing she could do to escape. The leader stepped forward and ripped her clothes off, starting with her blouse, then he feasted his eyes on her naked body. "Oh I can just jump your bones," he said stroking her breasts. Then he took his boots off and started pulling his pants down.

All his gang members had pretty much forgotten about the rest of the friends lying on the floor and were crowded around the table leering. They didn't see PJ crawl into the room with a hunting knife in his hand and cut the zip tie from Dale's wrists. PJ stood up slowly and took a couple of quick steps over to the nearest gang member who was standing a bit behind all the others with his hands fondling his crotch. In one movement he put his hand over the guy's mouth and simultaneously slit his throat. By now the rest of the gang was crowded around the leader and making a lot of noise as the leader prepared to mount Sam. At this point they were taking no notice of anything else.

Big mistake. PJ lowered the guy to the floor as his body went limp. Then he gave Dale the knife and Dale started releasing everyone. Meanwhile PJ grabbed the dead man's hand gun, stood up and immediately started pumping rounds very deliberately into the heads of all the gang members. Pow! Move to new target. Pow! Next target. Pow! Now YOU. Pow! This was all going on in slow motion in PJ's eyes but back in the real world, in real time, the gang never stood a chance. PJ's movement and shooting were like lightning. Their deaths happened so fast that their bodies didn't even twitch; they were just lifeless pieces of meat hitting the ground.

The leader had just started to get on top of Sam when the gang members holding her arms and legs had their heads blown off by PJ. The leader went for a knife strapped to his right leg above his ankle but as he was about to stick it in Sam she bit his left arm and grabbed his knife hand. He yelled and almost dropped the knife. Now she pulled him down on her with her right hand cupped around his neck and slammed him in the face with her forehead and then kneed him viciously in the groin. This caused him to finally drop the knife and roll off the table onto the floor, doubled up in agony! While all the shooting was going on, Dale was still cutting the zip tie off Jeff but Kacie had got her hands on Dale's thirty-ought six. While PJ blew the last gang member away, Kacie loaded a round and holding the rifle at waist-height pointed it at the half-naked leader as he staggered up from the floor and backed away from her. Kacie's face was awful to see, she could have been the reincarnation of that most feared pirate of the Caribbean; Blackbeard, his face ghostly and white-rimmed with smoke from the burning fire-crackers tied into his long black hair. The leader was staring at her and backing away slowly, already knowing he was looking at his death. His eyes flicked to his assault rifle lying on the table where Sam had been.

"Go for it." said Kacie with nothing but blackness in her eyes. He went for it and as he did this Kacie pumped a round into his chest. BAM! And his body slammed backwards onto the floor spurting blood. "Geezus this thing's got a kick like a mule!" exclaimed Kacie.

It was over so quick. Just a mess of bodies and blood, with the friends standing around rubbing their wrists where the zip ties had been, all still in shock. The girls helped Sam get some clothes on. PJ picked up an M16 lying against the wall and grabbed all the clips he could find off of the bodies splattered around. "I'm going to hang on to this, it looks like we could do with a bit more fire power." No one looked surprised, in fact, everyone was in such a state of shock that they were pretty much walking around like they were half-dead. They left the bar area, and the bodies where they had fallen in pools of blood, and headed off into one of the living quarters. June and Kacie made some coffee and tea but it took them all a long time before they had recovered enough to talk normally. "Geezus PJ," said Dale, "where the hell did you learn to shoot like that?"

"I nearly got killed once by a gang in Africa," replied PJ, "so I guess because of the way I handled myself and managed to escape, the police gave me a licence to carry a concealed firearm. Never got to use it in anger but I ran through six shots on a shooting range so I knew which end was which," he paused.

"But it wasn't that experience that counted today. Taking out those guys was more like racing motorbikes than you might imagine. At the most extreme limits my brain seems to speed up. It's not a conscious thing, I've no control over it. But in those fractions of a second before my, well what my subconscious figures is likely to be my death, I guess; everything slows down ten or maybe twenty times and I have time to at least know what I should be doing. Perhaps I can actually do it. I'm not sure. It's a bit like living in a dream."

"Some dream!" said June quietly.

PJ was still trying to explain and staring off into his world from long ago. "I've been on the grid of several fairly high profile road races on a Grand Prix bike, where people have spent a whole bunch of dough to get me there and I'm expected to win. I always did, but it was never easy. You have to clamp your mind in a vise and put yourself on a knife-edge. If you blow it and crash at those speeds, there's no guarantee you're going to wake up. So," he paused, "no mistakes, there's no second chance; and there is no other possible outcome but winning." Everyone was looking at him. "This was the same... there was no alternative. I just did what I had to do, perfectly. I'm so glad I got it right."

"PJ," said Andy quietly. "we owe you, big time."

PJ just nodded and a rather tired smile flickered across his face. Then Andy turned to Kacie and said: "You were wicked with that thirty-ought six."

"I was in a fighting mood," replied Kacie grimly.

"I'm sure glad both of you are on our side!" said Dale with a bit of a wry smile. Now they all began to relax. PJ went up to Sam who was sitting down recovering, put his hands on both her shoulders and said quietly: “I’m so glad you’re all right.”

“Thank you so much,” whispered Sam and touched him on the hand.

But now PJ really blew it; he looked at Sam and said; “Well at least those guys had good taste...”

There was a stunned silence, both electric and oppressive like the hot and muggy air before the monsoon breaks. It was like a row of thunderclouds had suddenly appeared all around him, and there was no time between now and the flash of light, thunderclap and deafening roar of torrential rain.

“It’s a joke,” PJ said quickly.

But the silence continued only for a fraction of a second before it was broken by Marie walking up to him and punching him in the face while simultaneously two of the other women started beating on him. PJ covered his head with his arms and yelled “Pax, pax,” and eventually the pounding stopped; the thunderclouds had gone leaving just the water covering everything and rushing off to hide deep inside the earth. He raised his head with one eye starting to swell up and blood dripping from a cut on his lip.

“Geez PJ,” said Kacie (who hadn’t taken part in the beating), “you really say the dumbest things.” She gave him some tissues to mop the blood up with and then said: “What’s Pax?”

“It’s Latin,” mumbled PJ with his fat lip, “and in this case it means don’t beat on me I’m just a wuss!”

When things had calmed down again PJ said: “Oh, you’ll never guess what happened to me at the chalet!” Then he told them of his narrow escape.

“The worst part was having nothing to defend myself with when I left my pack and bow in the bedroom, I was naked effectively. They were just going to kill me anyway they liked. I remember thinking: 'If only I had a stick'. It was a really bad scene."

"Son of a bitch what is it with this place," exclaimed Tim. "Did all the inmates escape from the loony bin and come here?"

"These must have been the dregs from the gangs on the coast," said Dale. "Out in the country like this they must have been bored out of their minds!"

"How many were down there attacking you PJ?" asked June.

"I'm not sure, five maybe six."

"You think they'll come up here and try again?" asked Wendy.

"I don't know, but I don't think so."

"All the same," said Dale, "we should keep watch."

"I'm real happy they were such lousy shots," PJ said.

"So am I!" said Wendy, kissing PJ on the cheek and hugging him. This time PJ had no problem hugging her back!

"I don't think we should hang around here," Jeff suggested. "Maybe get an hour or two's rest then head out."

"We need to put someone on watch right now," said Andy.

"I'll take the first stint," offered Jeff.

"I'll keep you company, I can't sleep," added Heather.

Tim laughed. "Hey you two, no nookie, this is serious!"

"Right," said Jeff, and he and Heather walked outside holding hands.

"The sooner we can get down south," said PJ. "The sooner we can get things planted and growing... Oh bollocks, I left my sleeping bag down at the chalet, I have to go back and get it."

"No need," June replied. "We have a couple of spare sleeping bags at home. We must stop by our place anyway. We've got gas there and Andy and I need to get some stuff together."

"We need to fit four of our bikes up like yours to carry spare cans and gear," said Andy. "Actually getting south from our place may be a problem. The San Andreas fault blew up real bad down by Palm Springs. We'll have to keep east."

"We going east at Bakersfield anyway to see if we can find an old girlfriend of mine," said the Boneman.

"Weren't there a bunch of quakes all the way up to San Francisco?" asked Dale.

"Yes," replied Andy. "Not just on the San Andreas, some of the other fault lines had major quakes as well. We felt them where we were."

"They were scary," added June. "Everything was shaking. Things fell off the shelves. The ground outside was like the sea, going up and down like a deep ocean swell. Imagine that, the ground moving like the sea. Makes you wonder how permanent everything really is."

"Reckon some of the roads will be pretty bad in places," said Andy.

"Sounds like we're gonna have to do some bushwhacking," said PJ.

"We are that," replied Andy. "We'll head down I-80 to Auburn, and then cut across through Placerville on 49—that's the way we came up. We should be OK on 49 through to San Andreas and then it's just a short jog to our place."

The road leaving the ski lodge at the top of Donner pass

They left the ski lodge early, having slept only an hour or so. Andy and June led the way in the van, which was good, because finding 49 in Auburn was real tough. You had to go through the centre of town and making the correct turns on all the right streets was pretty tricky.

Highway 49 was a real canyon scraper with some of the tightest hairpins any of them had ever seen and 20 mph corner warning signs that actually meant 20 mph! PJ had done a lot of motorcycle riding on the road and one of his rules of thumb was that he could go round a corner twice as fast as a warning sign said. Not here poo-poo! Here you go over the edge into the canyon and a world of hurt if you try that nonsense! He was having a hard time and scaring himself just trying to go as fast as the signs. “I must be getting old!” he said to himself. But what a trip! It was a blast laying the bike over and scraping the footpegs on nearly every turn for mile after mile.

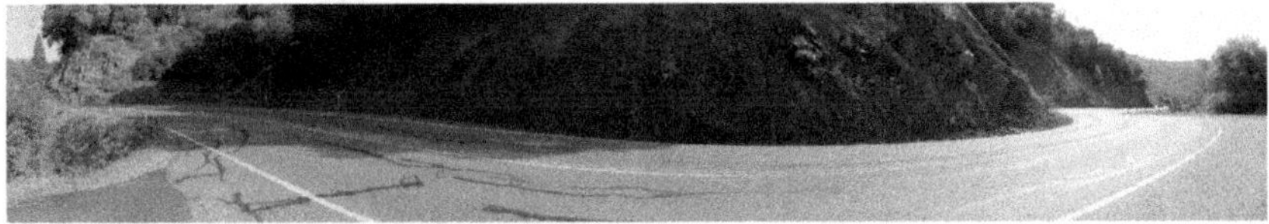

Highway 49 near Auburn

Where the roads opened up a bit after Placerville it reminded PJ of the roads south of London in Kent... tight and twisty with trees hanging over the roadway. There was no sighting around the corners so you never knew what was coming at you. But the trees here were wrong. This wasn't the old country, these were American trees. Funny that, no matter how similar a different part of the world is to where you used to live, it's still not home. South of Placerville they had trouble. A semi had jackknifed and was straddling a bridge. There was no way round through the fields and no side roads.

Andy got out of the van and looked at the semi. "We're not going to move that baby. I guess the team van is pants." Every-one except PJ and June was looking at Andy wondering what the hell he was talking about.

'American trees'

"He means it's no use any more," explained June. "We could maybe find another way around. But we'd have to go back. It would be a lot more miles, and there's no guarantee that those other roads would be open."

"Oh well..." said PJ. So they offloaded four of the bikes from the van and left it behind. They were able to drag all the bikes under the trailer of the crashed semi and then they headed off on the short ride to Andy and June's home. There they spent two days working on the bikes, doing maintenance and checking them out. Tim and the other guys set up four of Andy's bikes with extra gas cans and racks to strap stuff on the back while Marie got her first aid stuff and checked out the bullet wound in Andy's left leg. "You're lucky it missed the bone."

"Still hurts like hell, but I reckon I can ride OK if it doesn't start bleeding again."

"You should be all right. Looks like it's mending well. I'll strap it up with a straight splint for now but you just take it real easy and don't use that leg for anything. I'll strap it differently before we leave so you can ride with your knee bent."

The girls spent most of their time in the kitchen fixing food for the road, and going through June's wardrobe sorting out what June should bring with her.

"You have some real nice clothes," said Wendy. "I had to leave all my good dresses behind."

"I just had time to get my warm stuff," added Heather wistfully. "I was desperate to catch up to you guys!"

June smiled. "I have a ton of clothes, you all take whatever you want."

So it was a bit like Christmas, their birthday, and a party all at once with the girls and some of the guys too, choosing what they needed from Andy and June's extensive wardrobe.

"What about bike gear?" asked Andy. "We've got a bunch of the latest hot new stuff from Europe."

"It won't be any good once we have to start walking," replied Kacie looking through the racks of competition pants and team jerseys. "Sure is nice gear though."

Meanwhile, PJ had still not recovered from being beat up by

the girls; he was feeling bitter and annoyed with Marie and had been very quiet and keeping to himself.

"You're going to have to get over it eventually," suggested Kacie.

"I guess," replied PJ with a bit of a growl in his voice, "but this is how I deal with life; I opt out." Kacie just shook her head and walked away.

They planned on heading through Bakersfield to Barstow if the radiation levels from the LA area were low enough.

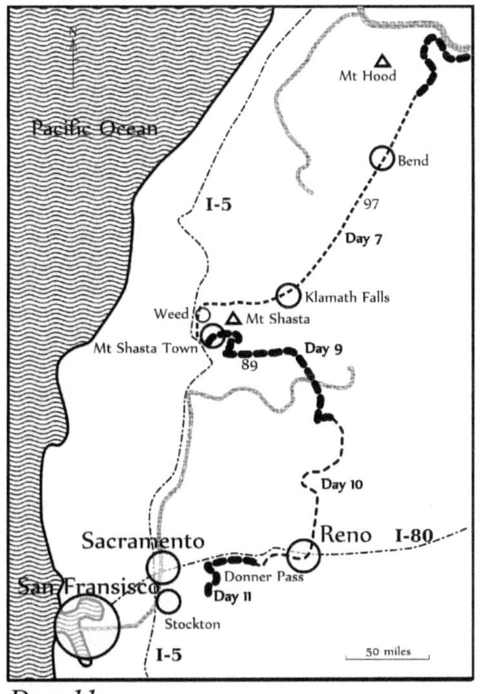

Day 11

"I guess it depends on what the wind was like when the nukes went off," said Jeff. "If the fallout went offshore it'll be OK going inland and around and down to somewhere near

Yuma. We'll be about 100 miles from ground zero."

"Yeah, smack in the middle of the worst part of the San Andreas fault!" said Andy.

"Only one way to find out," said Tim.

"I think we would be best to travel down 88 to Stockton and then take I-5 to Bakersfield," said Andy. "I-5 heads through more open country and there's a better chance we can make it through."

So the convoy headed out west and made their way through the garbage and wrecks that littered the roads in Stockton.

"This place was already a bit of a dump even before the nukes went off," said Andy.

"Yes," added June. "The city really made a bollocks of their finances."

But the friends got through OK by taking to the footpaths and dodging this way and that, squeezing the bikes through all the mess.

As Andy had guessed I-5 was pretty clear and there were only a few places where they had to cross over the median and ride on the opposite lanes. "Nice not having to worry about the CHP trying to trap us!" said Andy.

"Yeah, pity we can't cruise any faster than 45 loaded like this!" said Jeff.

Even with a following wind they could only get up to 50mph. Any sort of a hill or a headwind and they slowed to 35 or 40... absolutely crawling on these big straight interstates. They were built for the average Joe to do 75 mph eating a hamburger and fries with the kids watching a movie. They didn't push it because at the slower speeds there was a huge saving in fuel consumption, and anyway, what would they want to rush for? There was a finish line, sure, but this was the last race, and for once every finisher got to win.

But despite Andy's prediction, I-5 turned out to be a death trap about 60 miles after it was joined by the freeway out of San Francisco. As they crested a rise they could see the mess; mile after mile of wrecks stretching all the way to the horizon on both sides of the freeway. It was a war zone and when they got to it the stench from the rotting bodies was horrible even now, and there were still birds picking on the remains. Andy grimly started getting his bike through the wrecks while everyone else watched, then about a hundred feet in he started to cross over the median to where there appeared to be more of an opening on the other carriageway.

PJ was still disgruntled so he stood back and watched while a couple of the others began to follow Andy. Then he said loudly: "When you stupid buggers have figured out that you're going to end up like those corpses trying to get through that lot, you can follow me, I'll wait for you at the turn off."

"You know a way to bypass this?" asked Heather.

But PJ had already turned away and didn't reply; he just rode off back the way they had come.

"Fuck," said Kacie, "we better follow him, I think he knows what he's doing."

She was in a bad mood and thoroughly annoyed with the way PJ was carrying on. They called out to Andy to stop and Jeff walked over to him to explain what PJ was doing.

"He's going to cut across to 99," said Andy. "Actually that's a pretty good move, we should do it."

PJ was waiting at the top of the freeway on-ramp for a minor road about three miles back. "All those people that died back there? Lemmings," he said to no one in particular, "they didn't think, they just followed what the majority was doing. What the hell; the good, or maybe it's just the lucky ones, survive."

When everyone had got there he led them off east, crossing through the farm land of the San Joaquin valley. As they travelled there was a lovely scent of roasting almonds and pistachios from the plantations on either side of the road, a smell that wasn't there on I-5. It helped to lift their spirits a little. The road made several 90 degree turns, at one point heading them back north for a few miles, which was a little scary. But soon enough they turned east again and about an hour later arrived at 99. As PJ had guessed, it was almost free of wrecks even when they passed by the city of Fresno. Just before Fresno the scent in the air changed to something slightly acidic, perhaps that of grapes or some other fruit being dried. It was a nice counterpoint to the aroma of roasting nuts.

The gorge

At Bakersfield they headed off into the Greenhorn mountains on Highway 178. As they left the plains they entered a spectacular gorge with a clear flowing stream just below the road.

It was the perfect place to spend the night and a very relaxing end to a long, slow, and pretty miserable day.

Sacramento
Reno
I-80
N
Stockton
San Francisco
Day 14
I-5
Fresno
Kernville
99
Lake Isabella
Bakersfield
Los Angeles
I-10
Palm Springs
Salton Sea
San Diego
I-8
Tijuanna
Mexicali
US
Mexico
Highway 1
San Felipe
Pacific Ocean
Campo Grande
50 miles
Baja

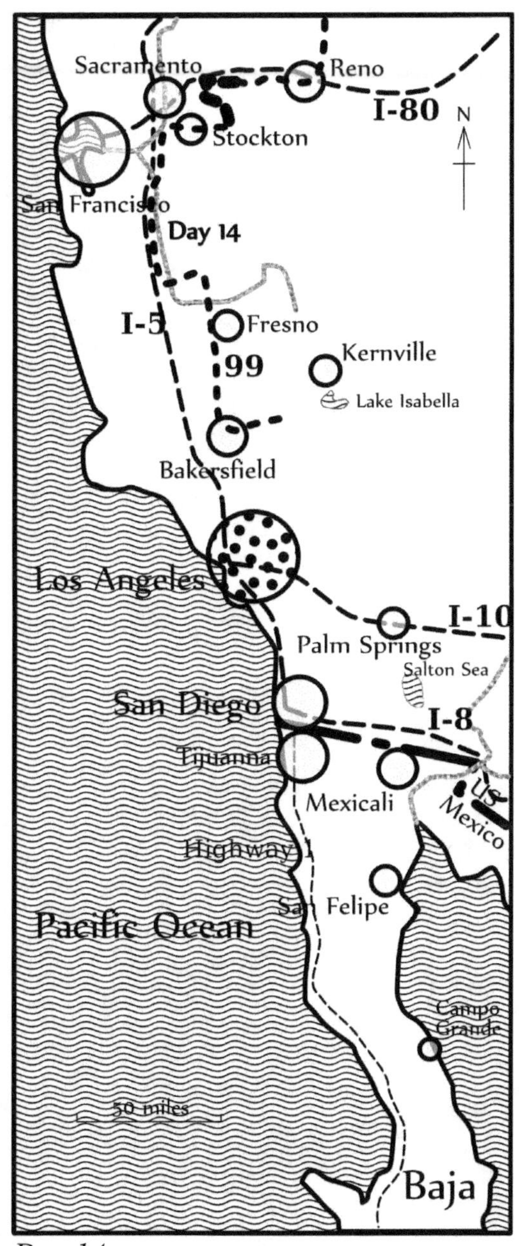

Day 14

Chapter 11, Susan's Place.

Lake Isabella

The next morning they carried on up the gorge and turned north when they got to the village of Lake Isabella, travelling round the western edge of the lake itself. At the northern end of the lake they got to Kernville which was where Susan lived.

There they had to go through an unmanned roadblock at the entrance to the village. The roadblock was built like a chicane so you could drive through it but you had to slow right down. It was a bit creepy and PJ felt like something was wrong. But nothing happened, just like all the other roadblocks except for the one at Mt. Shasta.

The Shell station at Kernville

Nonetheless the sound of the bikes' exhausts crackling and reverberating against the steep rocky hill on the left of the road made him wish they had silent electric motors. On the other side of the road from the steep hill was a Shell service station. They usually looked for gas at stations like this but PJ waved at everybody to keep going. It just didn't seem like a good place to hang around.

Susan's house was only a short distance away. When the Boneman led them there they parked the bikes and as they headed towards the door a frightened face appeared at the window. First just from the eyes up, then the whole face and then the look changed to amazement. By the time Susan had the door open she was as happy as Larry: as happy as she had ever been, and she was hugging everyone, but especially the Boneman!

"How did you get through the roadblock at the village?" asked Susan.

"There was no one there," replied Dale.

"Can they have gone? I've been a virtual prisoner here. They are such bad people—this gang that has taken over the village. They've been killing everyone. I've been waiting for them to come... here..." Susan's voice trailed off and she started shaking. The Boneman held her tight and patted her back until she had recovered.

"How are we going to get out of here?" asked Tim. "Is there a back road?"

"It's blocked up in the hills," replied Susan. "The only other road has a big slip that's washed it away right by the lake. We have to go out the way you came in."

"Do you have a motorbike?" asked Dale.

Susan shook her head. "Just the car. But it's electric and the batteries have gone flat."

"Oh bloody hell!" said PJ.

"I have a friend who has a regular car, I think he has gas. Maybe he will come with us?"

To find out, Heather took Susan on the back of her Beemer and together with PJ and Kacie on their bikes, drove up the road to her friend's place. Turned out her friend Alex had nearly a full tank of gas in his small car. Alex was twenty four and you bet your life he was real happy to come with them. They left him packing up and went back to Susan's place.

"Maybe we can get some ideas on how to get out of here if you show us where the gang is," said Jeff.

"They're at the Shell station," said Susan. "That's where they're holed up."

"Oops!" said PJ. "We got lucky there."

Susan led the men off up the hill at the back of her place and around on a path bypassing the houses below them. Then they looped back and scrambled through the dry scrub up the small hill next to the village. Dale had his thirty-ought six while Jeff carried Dale's large binoculars. Susan had a pair of wildlife binoculars.

The hill overlooking the Shell station

"We're in the Sequoia National Forest, aren't we?" asked PJ. "I thought there were these huge Sequoia trees here."

"Nope," replied Susan, "what you're thinking of is quite aways north. Eighty, maybe a hundred miles. It's called something else, Giant Sequoia National Forest I think, something like that."

"It's almost the dollar ninety nine trick," said PJ.

"What the hell are you talking about?" exclaimed Dale.

"Dollar ninety nine..." replied PJ, "You know, it's not two dollars. Get the suckers in the store!" Everyone else just shook their heads and sighed. PJ was being PJ.

About ten minutes later they crested the hill and had a good view of the valley. Down below them to their left was the steep slope overlooking the Shell station.

"We should be real careful as we get closer, it's quite steep," warned Susan.

They walked carefully down the hill until they had a good view of the service station then sat down and waited using the binoculars to check for any signs of life. Twenty minutes went by before they saw anything, then a woman walked past one of the windows inside and shortly two men came outside and took a leak against the side of the building. They looked pretty scruffy and they were obviously zonked.

"They're high," said Jeff.

"They're stoned," added Tim.

"Yeah, they're having a good time," agreed Dale. "That's good for us. They must have been out of it when we came into town. That's why we got through."

There was more movement inside seen through the windows. After an hour of watching they figured that there were eight people in the building, five men and three women. They had Harleys with high rise handlebars parked outside, which appeared to be their main wheels.

"We could lure them away," said Tim. "Get them to chase us while the others escape through the roadblock."

"Yeah but you're not going to get them all to chase us," said the Boneman. "What do you do about the others?"

"Firebomb them," replied Tim.

"Firebomb them?" asked PJ. "How are you going to do that?"

"Shoot the regulator off that propane tank and then fire a lighted arrow at it. Those still there won't be bothered about anyone passing through the roadblock, they'll be too busy trying to save their ass." There was a decent-sized propane tank next to what looked like a shop on the north end of the service station.

"How do we know there's propane in that tank?" asked Jeff.

"You can see the frost line if you look carefully with the binoculars," replied Dale.

"Oh yeah," said PJ. "Hmm. Anyone got any other ideas?" No one did.

"I can show you a trail that goes over the hills through some ranch country and down to the main road," offered Susan. "You can take the Harleys that way... they won't get through. It's pretty tricky to follow though, there are lots of trails all going different directions."

"I have a good memory for trails," said PJ.

"It brings you out on the main road about a half-mile or a mile out of town," Susan continued. "Depending on which trail you take. If you can actually get the Harleys to follow you on to the rougher part of the trail it'll take quite a bit of time for them to get turned round and come back."

"Any problem with getting our trail bikes through?" asked Tim.

"No, you'll be just fine," replied Susan.

"I wonder if those guys will just shrug it off?" said the Boneman.

"Y'know what," said Tim. "They'll chase us any way we go, if we do it right."

"What, flip them the bird?" Dale joked.

"Yeah baby!" said Tim seriously.

"Sounds like a plan," said Dale. "When do we do this?"

"Right before we're ready to leave," replied the Boneman.

"I need to get packed, what should I bring?" asked Susan.

"Just essential gear," Tim answered.

"Everything you need to live year-round," added PJ, "that you can carry on your back. At some point in time we're going to be walking."

"I have some hiking gear: pack, boots, and clothes," said Susan.

"Perfect."

"I also have a nice stainless cooking set that's real light and packs small."

"Don't forget wet and cold weather gear. We're going to be gone a long time!" said Jeff.

Susan smiled and looked at the Boneman. "I'm so glad you guys came." The Boneman was looking real happy too!

When Alex arrived they began loading Susan's stuff in his car. While this was going on Alex started chatting with Kacie and the two of them were hitting it off just great. Alex was really handsome, well muscled and fit, and Kacie was definitely attracted to him. However, Mike was taking notice. Abruptly he shoved all six foot of himself in-between them, grabbed Kacie by the shoulders and kissed her full on the lips. The effect on Alex was like stepping into a fancy restaurant wearing jeans and a T-shirt and being told by some officious prick that he needed a tie and jacket! For Kacie it was like kissing a large dead fish. Not quite what she had been working up to! "Still," she said to herself later, "better to get that out of the way early." Alex just brushed it off. He was at that stage in life where his strength and fitness gave him an almost irrepressible confidence in himself.

He made it up with Mike later. "Hey, sorry about that come on with your wife."

"No worries mate," replied Mike.

PJ borrowed Tim's big Yamaha trail bike because it had a decent passenger seat, and when Susan's stuff was loaded into the car she got on the back behind PJ and guided him over the route he had to follow to lead the Harleys into trouble. They had to go out down Susan's road and then left on another road up into the hills. There they turned left on a very narrow tarseal road that ended up at someone's house. At the back of the house they got onto a dirt road that led to an old barn. On the other side of the barn was a walking trail that headed down a steep slope into a gully. This walking trail was so rough and steep that Susan had to get off while PJ bulldogged Tim's bike down and then across a dry wash at the bottom.

"This'll stop the Harleys," said PJ. "Those suckers would have trouble with a wheelchair accessible path!"

"There's a way to get by this which is much easier," said Susan. "But those Harley guys won't know it. We'll go back the easier way."

The beginning of the Harley trap route

They followed the small walking path up out of the gully they were in, and then took the first of several different dirt tracks that were set up almost like a maze through the scrubby hills heading south towards the main road down by the river. A short while later they came out on the main road.

The maze of tracks

"Pity we couldn't get the car all this way," said PJ.

They turned round and headed back with PJ making mental notes of all the track junctions. "I'm going to have to get this right, there's no time for mistakes and having to backtrack."

It was early evening by now so they all decided to get a night's rest before making the escape bid.

After the evening meal PJ happened to be walking past one of the bedrooms when he heard the sound of crying. He stuck his head in the bedroom, and there was Sam sitting on the bed crying her heart out. He didn't have a clue what to do and was trying to work up the courage to go and comfort her when Kacie walked by.

"Don't do anything," she said.

PJ looked surprised. "Is it my fault?"

"No," said Kacie, "absolutely not, she's just having a good cry, she'll be fine afterwards."

PJ was still not convinced.

"I do it all the time," explained Kacie. "In fact all girls do it all the time. It's been a stressful few days, and when stress builds up it has to be released. Better out than in, I say. A boy would probably punch a wall. A girl will cry, and then she's perfectly fine afterwards... better even! Clear thinking and optimistic."

"You do this?" asked PJ.

"Oh sure. Like say at a national Trials event, it's a high stress situation. I want to win, but I've had some bad rides. Instead of carrying the bad rides with me I have a cry, let them go, and I'm back at the top of my game. It happens a lot, you've just never seen it because I go off the trail to be on my own."

"I've seen you come back on the trail," said PJ, "I just assumed you'd gone off for a pee!"

"Oh shush!" exclaimed Kacie.

Next morning it was another lovely California day with clear blue skies and mild temperatures. After everyone had a bite to eat and drink, Dale and the Boneman headed off to the top of the cliff where they would wait until the chase began. Alex had his car ready and the others were set to go on their bikes. They would wait for Dale and the Boneman to return.

Day 15

PJ and Wendy were the bait for the chase. These two had their bikes stripped down with their excess gear in the back seat of Alex's car. This way they would be as fast and nimble as possible. After thirty minutes had passed they figured Dale and the Boneman would be set up so they fired up the bikes and took off down the road towards the service station. On the top of the steep hill overlooking the service station Dale had set up his rifle, while the Boneman had climbed part way down and set himself up hidden at the top of a large rock outcrop where he was within arrow range. They had been waiting only a few minutes when PJ and Wendy rode their bikes down the road through the village and into view of the service station. There was a flurry of activity and the gang came running out as the two turned round in the road and stopped a few hundred feet away.

"Haven't you always wanted to do this to a biker gang!" said PJ with a wicked grin. Wendy laughed and with great deliberation the two of them turned round to face the Harley riders and gave them the finger.

This had a similar effect to poking a hornets' nest with a short stick! The whole gang went ballistic—shouting obscenities and waving their fists. Three of them leaped onto their Harleys and floundered around getting those unwieldy machines out onto the road after PJ and Wendy, who by now were well off back up the way they had come. The other two men and the three women watched and when the Harleys had disappeared they went back inside.

While all this was going on the Boneman had poured gas over some cloth tied to the head of one of his arrows. Now Dale took aim at the connection to the regulator on the propane tank. He fired three shots and nothing happened. "Goddamit. That sucker is tough." He carried on shooting and finally blew the regulator off with the sixth shot. The gunfire brought the two men back outside looking for action. Which was pretty stupid really... stepping into the open when someone's firing shots around. Meanwhile the Boneman lit his arrow and fired it off at the tank, then he ducked down behind the rocks.

The burning arrow made a beautiful sight as it arced silently through the air, then there was a flash of light followed by a huge explosion and the side of the building was partially collapsed and engulfed in flames. The men were stunned and knocked to the ground from the explosion. Then Dale took them both out with a couple of head shots. The Boneman scrambled up the hill to Dale and the two of them hightailed it back to Susan's place.

Susan and Heather had been around the back of her place on a walking path through some brush and trees. They were watching the road that the Harleys would take up into the hills. First came PJ and Wendy and then the three Harleys went thundering by. The two of them walked quickly back to her house and waited with everyone else. When Dale and the Boneman arrived everybody headed out to make their escape through the roadblock.

PJ and Wendy had reached the end of the tarseal road at the house and had the Harleys closing in on them as they went round the back and out onto the dirt track. Coming up to the old barn PJ uncharacteristically crashed on a turn. He lost his front wheel and slid out into the ditch. This was major panic time for PJ and he scrambled to get out from under the XT. He was trying to lift it upright when the Harley riders roared into sight with vengeance in their eyes.

Wendy reacted instinctively and motocrossed her way up the dirt bank doing a wheelie turn 20 feet past the top of the bank on the hillside. The wheelie turn brought her big Yamaha back facing down the hill and then she jumped the bike off the bank into the side of the lead Harley smashing it to the ground. She spun her bike round in the dirt and took aim at the next Harley who was slamming on his brakes. The third rider had already dumped his bike and was getting out of Dodge scrambling on all fours up the bank. The rider Wendy was heading at bailed when she came at him pulling a wheelie. He scrambled to his feet and headed up the bank after the other rider both of them completely forgetting that Wendy could ride up there! By then PJ had got his bike upright and fired up so Wendy joined him instead and the two of them raced off. On the other side of the barn they disappeared down the very rough walking track heading into the gully. This time PJ didn't get off and bulldog his bike and he and Wendy had a really wild scary ride to the bottom both of them barely able to stay on their bikes. But the Harley rider that Wendy had originally smashed into had picked his bike up and got after them and was so mad at her that he followed them down. The other two Harley guys got back on their bikes and stopped when they got to the top of the walking track. There they watched as the third rider rapidly slid out of control down the gully, eventually high siding and tumbling together with his bike in a flurry of dirt and rocks and boulders three quarters of the way to the bottom. When the dust settled the two smart ones at the top saw the other guy was OK and turned round to head back to the service station. "He's not getting his bike out of there in a hurry. He can walk back," said one of them. "Serves him right for being so stupid!" said the other.

PJ and Wendy meanwhile had got to the bottom and were heading off up the other side of the gully towards the maze of dirt roads and tracks that would take them south to the main road. Coming up the other side there were a lot of loose rocks on the path and PJ gassed it early to get up a couple of rock ledges that were sitting one on top of the other. Keeping momentum and getting up tough climbs was one thing he was good at.

Wendy had been following a bit close so she stopped to see what she was heading into. PJ leaned his bike against a rock and went back to be ready to help if she had trouble. Surprisingly she did. She couldn't get up enough speed on the rollers in the path and lunged at the ledges jumping off the bike with her hands still on the handlebars. But PJ was ready and grabbed one of the front forks and together they got the bike up just fine.

"You didn't have to do that," she said, which somewhat froze the smile on PJ's face! "But I like it that you did," she continued with a slight smile and PJ's face loosened up into just the tiniest part of a grin!

When they got all the way to the main road and shut their bikes down to wait for everyone PJ said: "Hey that was some riding you just did with that huge wheelie turn on the hillside. Man where did you learn how to handle a big off-road bike like that?"

"Endurocross," replied Wendy smiling. "If you can ride that you can jump tall buildings and maybe even fly to the moon!"

PJ laughed and the two of them high-fived.

Wendy explained her grumpiness at PJ catching her bike: "My dad used to always stand ready to catch me when I went up stuff. It was OK at first but then as I got older I started to resent it. I figured I knew what I was doing and although I was afraid of crashing I wanted to show I was just as tough as the boys. Eventually it was only the boys who could ride where I went and I didn't mind them catching me!"

"Well the only reason I went back to help you was because you're a girl!"

Wendy yelled and started beating up on PJ but he got a lock hold on her wrists and put his face close to hers. "Oh, what's that great perfume you're wearing?" he said with a sly grin.

"WD 40!" Wendy shouted back.

"Mmm, nice!"

Wendy wrestled her hands free, moved away from PJ, put her

hands on her hips, and twisted her body provocatively. "Hah. Men! Can't live with them—can't live without them!"

PJ just grinned.

A little later as they were sitting down waiting for the others Wendy said: "Don't worry about Marie, she'll get over it, she had a pretty rough time with Sandy's dad and got quite bitter."

PJ just smiled and shrugged his shoulders. "I don't get over things easy."

"Like not eating meat?" replied Wendy, "It's a luxury we can't afford..."

The service station was blazing fiercely as the convoy of riders approached with Alex and Susan following in the car. The three women from the gang were busy trying to salvage some stuff from inside and get it out of harm's way. They stopped to look as the convoy passed them and made its way through the roadblock.

Just then the two Harley riders appeared down the street after giving up on chasing PJ and Wendy. They roared up to the road-block and stopped. Then one of them leaped off, kicked his stand out and pulled a rifle from the gear bag on the back of his bike. He ran to the other side of the roadblock, kneeled down and aimed at the back of Alex's car, now a couple of hundred yards off heading down the road...

Chapter 12, Escape!

Alex and Susan were last through the roadblock in his car and Alex was looking in the rear-view mirror when he saw the guy with the rifle. He slammed his foot to the floor and continued looking in the mirror, mesmerised by what he was seeing. He saw the man kneel down and his right hand load the first round, then a pause and a puff of smoke. A second later there was a clang as the bullet hit the trunk of his car. The hand loaded the next round, another puff of smoke and Alex stiffened his body waiting for... CLANG, another hit. Again the man reloaded and again there was the silent puff of smoke followed a second later by the sound as the bullet hit the car. It was just like the movies only it was for real and they were both absolutely freaking out of their minds. Now Alex had to look ahead and steer to get around a wide corner and then they were out of sight of the man with the gun, and safe.

"Are you all right?"

"Yes, how 'bout you?"

"I'm OK. Whoo, that was about as close as it gets!"

They all met half a mile down the road where PJ and Wendy were waiting for them. There they checked the car real quick.

"Pretty good grouping!" said Dale and he put his right hand with the fingers spread out over the three bullet holes. They found no serious damage, the clothing and camping gear in the boot had soaked up the bullets so some of the clothes had holes in them.

"Clothes we can fix," said Kacie. "I'm real glad you guys are OK."

"It was pretty freaky," replied Susan.

“I can imagine,” said Kacie. “The bastards!”

They headed off to the village of Lake Isabella at the southern end of the lake and then up into the Piute Mountains, to a small valley where Susan thought they might be able to get gas at a freind’s farm. It was a pretty scary road in places with huge drop-off’s and no guard rails.

The Piute Mountains

There was no one at the farm but they found a couple of dirt bikes and some farm equipment still with gas in them. They pottered around making some temporary panniers for the two dirt bikes and while all this was going on Marie checked out the bullet wound Andy had got at Donner Pass. “It’s healed nicely. How does it feel?”

“Just fine. No pain at all but my calf muscle is still a bit stiff.”

“I think you’re good to go. Maybe do some stretches every time we stop.”

“Will do!” said Andy grinning.

There were a couple of wind chimes on the veranda of the house playing their tinkling metallic song in the gentle breeze. But as they listened they had the strangest feeling... like they were being watched, but there was no one else to be seen. Then something flickered in the corner of Kacie’s eye. She looked at the house. “I think there’s someone in the farmhouse.”

“Susan and I checked it when we arrived,” said Mike.

“There was no one there,” added Susan. “It’s empty.”

"You checked the kitchen?" asked Kacie.

"Actually," replied Susan. "It's a bit funny but the kitchen did look as though it was being used. I thought it looked a little odd. It didn't have any dust and it was neat and tidy." She paused. "There was no one there though."

The farm in the Piute mountains

The wind chimes kept playing as everyone stood still, looking and listening. All the while Kacie was staring at the upper windows. Suddenly she rushed towards the house and went inside and up to the top floor. The others stood still while Mike ran after her. When they came back they had two scared kids with them, one walking holding Mike's hand, the other cradled in Kacie's arms. The kids eyes were wide open and they were quite frightened. Everyone stopped what they were doing and went inside the farmhouse, where the girls cooked up some food as they all talked to the kids.

"Where were you hiding?" asked Susan. "We looked."

"Under the bed!" said the girl.

"Oh we didn't think of looking there!" said Mike.

"Good hiding place!" said Tim.

"What are your names? How old are you?" asked Kacie.

"Evelyn, my friends call me Evie and this is my brother Will, I'm 8," replied Evie.

"My names William, and I'm 6," said Will, standing up very straight and stiff with his chin tilted slightly up. Some of the guys had to cover up a smile with their hand; he was so very serious!

"William; Will and Evie. Hey, you're two tough cookies living here alone." said Jeff. "What happened to your parents?"

"We don't know," replied Evie. "They never came back."

"How long have you been alone?" asked Dale.

The kids just stood there looking at them. They shook their heads. They didn't know.

"It must have been a long time," said Susan, "I remember your parents worked in LA some of the time. Perhaps they were there when the nuke went off. I wish I'd known you were here, I would have come and got you so you could stay with me."

Evie was holding some knitting tight against her upper body. "That's nicely done," said Kacie touching the knitting, "do you like knitting?" Evie nodded.

Will was looking a bit defiant and standing a little apart from everyone. Mike turned to him. "And what do you do Will?"

"I look after my sister!"

Actually it looked like Evie could look after herself but that was beside the point. Will knew his role in life!

Everyone was looking admiringly at these two tough little survivors. "Well you two better come with us, we think we can live out the winter in Mexico. You good with that?" asked Kacie. The kids nodded, their eyes not so wide open now, but the mugs of hot stew in their hands were shaking a little in the warm California midday, as though their hands were cold as ice.

"Hey guys," said Jeff. "We gotta fix up some way to carry these two."

"How do we do this?" asked Tim.

"Well, I reckon I can carry one in front of me on the gas tank if we strap on some sort of seat," said Dale.

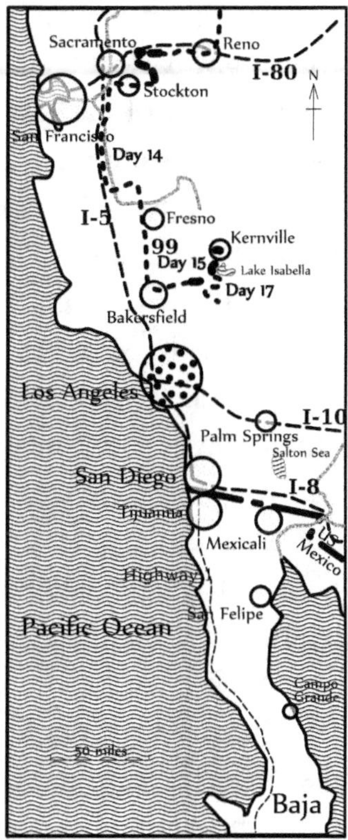

Day 17

"I can do that on the Beemer as well," added Heather.

So that's what they did using stuff they found in the farm workshop. They drained the farm vehicles of gas and then they siphoned Alex's car dry enough to refill all of their bikes. Every can they carried was topped up now.

It was late afternoon so everyone decided to spend the night at the farmhouse. After their evening meal Andy said: "We better put someone on guard overnight. We don't want another surprise attack."

"I'll take the first watch with Evie and Will," volunteered Kacie. While they were on guard Kacie showed the two kids how to use her bow and although neither of them were strong enough to pull the string right back, they still both hit the spot Kacie had marked out on the side of the barn.

The next morning when they were ready to leave, on impulse PJ took down the two wind chimes and stowed them in his pack.

"What are you going to do with those?" asked Jeff.

"Oh, you'll see!" replied PJ.

They left Alex's car with the three bullet holes in the trunk, at the farm and hit the road south. The kids were looking totally thrilled, sitting high up on the seats on the gas tanks with wide smiles on their faces, all wrapped up in thick warm clothing.

"Hang on tight!" said Dale as they started off.

Dale and Heather took it easy, cornering gently and being real careful on acceleration and braking. Neither of them were the risk-taking type and having the kids along for the ride was real fun for them. They chatted with the kids as they rode and pointed out neat things and what you had to do to ride the motorcycles, how to use the throttle and the clutch. The kids held on to the tank packs in front of them and soon got the hang of leaning with the bike on the corners of the winding and twisting narrow mountain road. The road was going down now all the way to the main dual carriageway that headed east out of Bakersfield.

On the dual carriageway as they got near the desert there were forests of windmills lining the sides and tops of the hills; some of them had crashed to the ground while others had broken and snapped off or were leaning at a crazy angle. And yet most of them were doing just fine and still turning slowly and lazily as if they had all the time in the world. Further away there was a whole string of smaller windmills moving much faster, revolving furiously, defiantly against the wind.

The windmills

"Generating clean and friendly power. For whom?" thought PJ. As they approached one of the nearer wind farms they could see that the laminations on one blade on one of the machines had torn and was hanging loose. The tear was about one third of the way down the huge blade. Even as they watched the tear became larger until the blade broke at the tear and arced up into the sky in a final beautiful moment of freedom before embedding itself into the hillside. Now the rest of the whirring mass was immediately out of balance, convulsing and shaking wildly in its death throes. A few brief seconds later the head ripped off and all the rotating parts were thrown to the ground in a mass of twisted metal, fibreglass and flying clods of earth and stone.

"Whoa dude!" said PJ.

California desert

Many hours later they got out of the hills and onto a huge desert plain. The road was now going straight as an arrow into the horizon and PJ was trying to check his map but in the bright sunlight his eyes had fatigued so bad they wouldn't focus that close. More miles went by and that old sinking feeling was sweeping through him. “We must have passed the turn off,” he said to himself. “I was looking so hard, how could I have missed it?” He signalled to the others to stop and got the map out from under the clear plastic. “Damn,” he thought to himself. “Why didn’t I make a note of the mile marker back at the last junction?” These maps weren’t that reliable, roads were always being re-built, or re-aligned. Maybe it had actually been at that last junction... or even perhaps you had to take the other road first? But there was no going back now, they didn’t have the gas to spend it on backtracking.

Distant hills north and south

He looked all around. There was nothing except distant hills north and south, and desert. He left the others and began to walk east towards something in the distance by the road. It took a long time to get there and when he did... it was just another abandoned vehicle, but no bodies this time, they would probably be further up the road either singly or in a group. That was how it worked. They drove until they could go no further then they walked until they dropped. And then their corpses were picked at by the birds and coyotes and the sun and wind until only bones and scraps of clothing remained. He knelt down and tapped the gas tank on the car. It was dry. He looked back and the others were just a speck in the distance. Just like in the Sahara, you could walk as far as you wanted but there was still nothing, no change, just the same desert—and when you looked back there was a speck in the distance where you had been; that was your friends, that might just as well be you.

PJ turned slowly around, searching for anything that stood out on the horizon that he could reference on the map. There was nothing. He took a deep breath, shrugged his shoulders and said: "Oh well..." and walked back to the others. They could see in his face what he was going to say. "We have to go on. I think we missed the turn off. There's another in about 30 or 40 miles." PJ looked around at everybody, they were tired and scared though they were trying to look calm. This was a very lonely place to be lost.

Only Kacie was really succeeding in covering up her true feelings. "PJ," she said, "we're following you." PJ gave her a rather tired smile to say thanks.

In strong contrast to everyone else, Evie and Will were not looking scared at all; it was one of the big advantages of being a child... you trusted the adults. Right up to the point sometime in your early teens, when you saw these gods who always looked after you make their first mistake. That was when you grew up and the world became a scary place to be. Right now the two kids were real happy being looked after, being fussed over and made to feel real special. And why not? Fairytales and magic kingdoms are to be treasured and enjoyed while you can.

"We have to go this far east anyway," explained PJ, "so the miles are not wasted." No one looked him in the eye and no one spoke. They got on their bikes and waited for him to lead.

It took them nearly an hour and it was a very long hour but they came to the junction with the other road at last. There were the remains of a service station, some fast food places and a few other derelict buildings. Here at last they turned south. They all had a better feeling now but no one more so than PJ... he was back on track! “This will take us down through Victorville,” he said, “then we can see what the superslab looks like and either take it through San Bernadino or head southeast on a smaller road.”

At the junction PJ hung up one of the wind chimes down low in a corner of one of the wrecked buildings. “To welcome us back on the return journey.”

“It’ll have a tough time lasting in the wind out here,” said Tim.

“I think it’ll be all right, but if it doesn’t last, well that’s OK,” PJ said shrugging his shoulders. “We’ll call this the wind chime corner.”

“Nice idea,” said Jeff.

PJ had been checking his Geiger counter once they had got on to the dual carriageway heading west but there was only a very low level of background radiation. “I’m guessing it’s going to be OK heading south now but I’ll keep checking.”

The camp site with the mountains way in the distance

The road was going almost directly south. It was dead straight and boring as all get-out at the slow speed they were doing. It was getting on towards evening so about seven miles later they stopped at the top of a small hill to camp. They headed off the road about 100 yards, slipping and sliding in the loose sand and dirt until they were the other side of some power line pylons.

There they camped on the flat top of a rise looking out over the desert. Later, after it had got dark, they sat around the fire talking, letting their food settle down. The night was clear with no moon, but the stars provided a full view of the desert they were travelling through. They could just see in the distance the 11,000 foot mountains of the San Bernadino national forest that they were heading towards. Kacie and Mike were talking to Alex about his work. He had been a storyboard artist working with some of the smaller Hollywood productions. He had even worked on some of the films that Sam had been in.

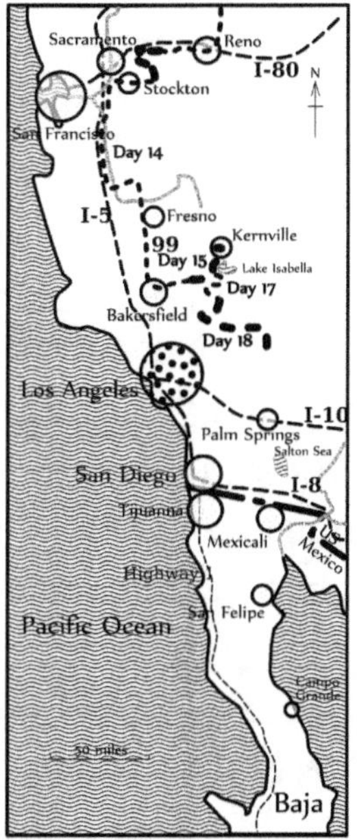

Day 18

“Do you do other stuff as well?” asked Kacie.

“Only pretty women!”

Everyone laughed, even Mike.

In the dark quiet early morning Jeff got up to take a leak, the moon had come up—and as he was standing there something caught his eye in the moonlight. It was like a shadow had moved in the distance. He zipped up his pants and just stood there looking, but nothing moved so as the cold night air started to seep into his body he went back to his sleeping bag under the stars. As he lay there getting ready to go back to sleep, his body electrified... he saw a shadow move again, and then another, and then several shadows all moved at once. Whatever caused them was perfectly camouflaged within the landscape of grey and black rocks, moon shadows and starlight—only the shadows could be seen moving one by one, closer and closer; like a silent trickle of water in the dry dusty earth hinting the start of a mighty flash flood.

He propped himself up on his elbow and started waking everyone up. "There's something coming at us," he whispered, "I don't know if it's people out to rob us or animals looking for a meal, either way I think we're under attack."

"We better get the hell out of here," said Dale.

Quickly everyone got their riding gear on and packed up their kit, and all the while in the distance they could see the shadows moving closer, although they were still several hundred yards away.

"Is everyone ready?" said PJ quietly.

"Yes" came the chorus of whispered replies.

"OK guys let's go!"

They started up their bikes and got them back through the sandy tracks on to the road in a confused flurry of sound breaking out loudly into the quiet desert night. Then they took off south on the long straight road. Behind them the shadows had stopped moving and had morphed into black statues all watching them ride away into the distance. Now the statues turned around and disappeared back into the black shadows of the night.

The air was bitterly cold in their faces, but the thought of what lay behind them added a layer of insulation to their body and a clarity of purpose to their mind. PJ was keeping a watch behind and a few minutes later his worst fears were realised... there were lights in the distance behind them, four wheelers. He passed everyone and signalled them all to gas it.

The road had several places where severe erosion from flood waters had washed it away. The second one they came across was real bad and some vehicles had made tracks off to one side into what was now a dry wash. But even these tracks had been washed away right at the bottom where it was very rough. They got all the bikes through OK but the Boneman and Heather needed help getting their machines through the loose sand and rocks at the bottom and up the other side. Heather and Dale let the two California kids Evie and Will off their bikes and these two scampered across on foot. Everything was shades of grey and black in the moonlight and they found it quite difficult keeping their balance in the loose dirt and sand. The yellow shafts of light from their headlights flickered up and down and every-which-way sideways as the front wheel bumped and turned, and it actually made things worse, just adding to the confusion of shapes and shadows for their eyes. A couple of miles later they stopped, and Dale and PJ sent everyone on ahead with instructions to keep going no matter what happened. Dale had swapped bikes with Tim so that Evie could go with them. As the others rode off the two of them walked back to where they could see the gully with the washout. They didn't have long to wait before one pair of headlights appeared and stopped on their side of the washout.

"They've gone back to help the other vehicles," said PJ.

"The washout isn't going to stop them," said Dale, "we better catch up to the others."

About ten miles further on it was starting to get light, but here they came across a roadblock. It was made up of abandoned vehicles shot through with bullet holes. When Dale and PJ arrived, most of the others had got past it without too much trouble by riding and pushing their bikes through the sand on the right side of the road. The other side was impassible as it had a whole bunch of vehicles that had tried to get through the loose sand and dirt and churned everything up into a morass. The vehicles had all been shot up. The sand on the right side was still a mess but the bikes could be ridden and pushed through it with a bit of effort.

After they had got past the roadblock, PJ and Dale stopped everyone about a mile up the road and told the others to go on.

"Wait when you get to the start of the built-up area near Victorville," said PJ, "there's a bunch of shops and fast food places on the right. Park out of sight, and keep a watch on the road for us. Don't go any further without us because we'll never find you in the maze of roads there," he paused, "We're going left at the road right after those shops but make sure you suss out an escape route ahead of time, because if it's not us but the four wheelers you need to know how to get out of there without having to think. OK?"

The roadblock was still in full view so PJ and Dale left their engines running. That way they could get away fast. Dale got out his binoculars and had his thirty-ought six ready to go. It took about half an hour before the four wheelers arrived at the roadblock.

"They've got a Humvee and some dune buggies and one of the buggies has got himself stuck in the sand where we got through," said Dale, "the others are trying to pull the wrecks out of the roadblock to make a gap. I think they're military, they've got uniforms."

"There's an airforce base not far away back the way we came," said PJ, "these guys must be survivors of that."

"Or thieves who've looted the base," said Dale. He picked up his thirty-ought six. "I'm going to give them something to think about," and he knelt down and pumped a round into the side door of the stuck dune buggy.

PJ was watching through the binoculars. "They've all taken cover, we should high-tail it out of here before they return fire."

"They won't follow us quite so closely now!" said Dale as they got back on their bikes and took off after the others again.

They caught up where everyone had hid their bikes out of sight behind the fast food places that were fronting the main road. Now PJ led them off left about 5 miles. They crossed I-15 and then eventually turned right onto Highway 18 and went through Apple Valley towards the village of Lucerne Valley. "If they decide to still chase us, hopefully they will think we've gone down I-15 to San Bernadino."

But no such luck, about 25 miles later they could see the headlights behind them again.

"Bugger," PJ yelled to Dale, "it didn't work. We're going to have to head for the hills. I know a very long and rough 'short-cut' that should give us an advantage and slow them down."

"Let's do it," Dale yelled back.

So PJ led everyone right off the main road and up towards Big Bear Lake on Highway 18. The sun was coming up on their left like a huge orange half-moon that quickly changed into a burning pale yellow globe. Now even their shadows chased them in the countryside beside them; long and black, flickering up and down on the bushes and grass and ground. It was a very anxious five or six miles on the flat straight road until they started to go up into the San Bernadino National Forest. The road up into the mountains was a real barnstormer with 10 mph hairpin corners and very steep grades all the way up to about 7000 feet. There was a great view of the plains behind them at the top but they didn't have time to stop and look.

The plains in the distance from the top of the 7000 ft pass

They drove down a short way towards Big Bear Lake then went left through the beginning of a small village. Now they turned off left again onto a dirt forestry road called 2N02. This soon began twisting and climbing up and down all over the place and was very rough. They were real slow on the dirt because of the two kids sitting on the gas tanks. After about eight miles of pounding along this road they dropped down and crossed a stream that was very rough and had about a foot of water.

The road leading out of the stream crossing

The track leading up the other side of the valley was extra bad where water had carved it away. They had to make a path in two places using rocks to fill in the worst of the erosion. After they had all got through Dale and Tim chucked most of the rocks back out of the washouts.

"Damned if I'm leaving them a good way to follow!" said Tim.

Half way up the other side they had a view of the stream crossing below.

"We need to buy some more time," said Dale to PJ.

The ambush spot with the stream crossing down below almost hidden by trees

So they sent the others on ahead with instructions to wait if they came to a junction. The two of them parked their bikes at the top, out of sight, and walked back to where they had a clear view of the crossing below them. Here they set themselves up, protected by some boulders, and just like before waited for about half an hour before they saw the vehicles that were chasing them cautiously approaching down the road.

"How the hell did they figure we had gone down this road?"

said PJ.

"Damned if I know!"

"Just the one shot again or shall we give them a bit more?"

"I don't think one will cut it this time."

So PJ readied the M16 he had picked up at Donner Ski Ranch and as the lead vehicle, the Humvee, got close to the stream the two of them opened up with a burst of rounds each. The Humvee immediately backed off out of sight as did the dune buggies. As the vehicles disappeared PJ and Dale high-tailed it back to their bikes and rode off after the others again.

The small plain up high in the San Bernadino national forest

It took over half an hour before they had caught up at a place where there was an especially rough uphill stretch of open rock on the track. As they got there Jeff was standing at the worst spot ready to lend a hand while Tim, Kacie and Wendy rode everybody's bikes up it. PJ and Dale got up without any trouble and then everyone carried on riding as fast as they could... which was not very fast for the Boneman and Heather who had to look out for the kids sitting on their tanks. Now they came to a small plain with a lot of Joshua Trees that PJ thought looked very much like the Giant Groundsel that grew high up in the mountains of East Africa.

Joshua Trees on the small plain

On the other side of the plain the forestry road briefly climbed a bit, then started the descent out of the mountains.

The forestry road going down out of the mountains

After an hour or so the road started getting better as it got lower on the southern side. Now they were able to travel faster but they knew the chasing vehicles would be able to speed up too. The road was still dirt and soft loose sand and quite tricky riding with their overweight bikes.

Scattered homesteads hidden amidst the Joshua Trees

About ten miles later they were still in the Joshua Trees in the valleys they were passing through, but some homesteads were starting to appear. Then the Joshua Trees gave way to farmland and more houses and shortly the road was tarseal again. Another seven or eight miles later they turned right onto Highway 62 which was the main road heading down to Palm Springs. 62 was a fast dual carriage way road with one particularly long straight stretch down and up out of a valley. As they got to the top on the other side, PJ looked back and there were the headlights of the chasing pack about eight miles away. Again he signalled everyone to gas it and they sped down out of the mountains on the last rather narrow pass before the plains around Palm Springs.

But now as they rounded the last corner and came onto the plains their whole world seemed to fall apart... They came across the San Andreas fault. It was as if a monster Caterpillar dozer half a mile wide and high had dragged its giant ripper blades across this edge of the valley plain. The road had been torn up into a tumbled mass of slabs of concrete and tarseal mixing into a turmoil of rocks and dirt stretching off on either side into the distance as far as could be seen.

"Oh shit," said PJ, "this must be why they are still chasing us... they know we can't get through."

"The fault starts at the Salton Sea," said Andy, "and goes right through Palm Springs. We're just on the northern side of it here."

"We're screwed," said Mike, "we'll never get the bikes through that before they catch us, what are we going to do now?"

Chapter 13, The Salton Sea.

The friends just stood there for a brief moment frozen in time staring at the mess. The road looked like the wreckers had had a go at it. There were big slabs of tarseal and concrete sticking several feet in the air and cracks and fissures everywhere. The destruction stretched off to the right and left of the road into the scrub and further off into the hills in the distance. Strangely though, it was only a quarter of a mile of the road that was torn up like this. They could see where the fault ended and the road was perfect once again.

"Come on, we've got to try to get across," yelled PJ as he began picking his way cautiously through the jumble and mess of rocks and slabs. Dale was right behind PJ but immediately recognised their danger and yelled. "We're not going to make it. I'm going back to buy us some time."

PJ waved to the others to keep going while he got his bike parked against a slab of concrete. "You need more firepower, we can make them slow down real good between the two of us."

Dale and PJ took their packs off, then they grabbed their rifles and ammunition and ran back up the road. They took cover behind the big concrete divider in the centre of the road and waited.

Back at the fault Tim and the Boneman were making a bit of a path for the bikes—filling in holes and gaps with rocks and rubble while behind them the others helped each other to walk and push all the bikes through. Towards the other side of the fault there was no way to get across a twenty foot deep ravine that had opened up, so in desperation everyone manhandled the bikes off the road a few hundred feet until they got to a spot where the steep edge had collapsed and they were able to bulldog the bikes down into the ravine. Now they needed a huge amount of effort to get each bike up the sheer dirt bank on the other side. But desperation breeds uncommon amounts of strength and resolve, so with everyone pushing, pulling and lifting and even standing on top of one another; one by one they got each bike and all their gear up the other side. The first few bikes were the hardest but then the lip at the top got rounded off as the dirt got kicked out by their feet and scraped by the machines so the rest of the bikes were a bit easier.

The tension was building for PJ and Dale as they looked back to see the painfully slow progress the others were making. And then it was too late... the dune buggies led by the Humvee appeared round the corner and were immediately in range so Dale put a couple of rounds into the Humvee. PJ let off a burst of fire at the lead buggy and the second buggy wasn't sure what was going on but got the message as PJ holed its radiator and steam shot out. All of them made a run to get off the road. Now they were out of sight in a shallow gully on the other side of the road and all they could see was a small plume of steam from where the buggy with the holed radiator was hidden. There was a short pause.

"I can see the top of the Humvee coming into sight," said Dale, then he paused as though he couldn't believe his eyes. "Oh shit they've got a big machine gun. Get down," he yelled.

There was a huge crackle of fire as tracer sped through the air above them and the massive rounds blasted big chunks off the concrete divider in front of them. The two of them cowered down, trying to force their bodies actually into the tarseal.

"Holy cow!" said Dale.

"Oh bloody hell!" added PJ.

There was a short pause, then another burst of fire from the Humvee.

"Goddamit, we can't fight that," said Dale.

"Shoot," agreed PJ, "Y'know, they're not going to come at us while they think were still here, it's too exposed. I'm going to get up the bank on the other side and then spray them with the M16 from above. You go back and get both our bikes across and then cover me from the other side of the fault while I make a run for it."

PJ and Dale crawled on their bellies over to the ditch on their side of the road and then used the ditch to keep hidden until they got back to the start of the fault. They were out of sight of the Humvee now and while PJ went back to climb the hill on the north of the road Dale started getting their two bikes across.

When he got to the other guys he said, "They've got a Humvee with a bloody great machine gun on the roof."

"Man we heard that," exclaimed Tim, "That is one big mean mother!"

"We caused them some damage," added Dale, "but that's nothing to what they'll do to us if they catch us still here!"

It was quiet when PJ got up the side of the hill, so he braced himself and then carefully and slowly raised his head to where he could see the top of the Humvee. He ducked down and looked back and saw all the bikes and gear were now up the other side of the ravine and everyone was riding off down the road. Most of the men had stayed behind to help get Dale and PJ's bike across. PJ slowly stuck his head up again and then quickly he sighted the M16 and let off the rest of the clip at the Humvee, seeing the sparks as his rounds hit the vehicle. Then he loaded another clip and sprayed the dune buggies. He ducked back down again just in time before the machine gun figured out where he was and opened fire on him. As the bullets zapped overhead and zinged off the rocks and ground he scrambled and slid his way down the hill. Then he ran through the mess of the fault zone down into the gully and scrambled up the other side with a helping hand from both Jeff and Alex. There Dale and Tim had his bike waiting for him with the engine running.

"We can't hang around," said PJ, "I don't know how much damage I did but that bloody great machine gun will rip us apart once they get us in sight."

Quickly they all got going, and it was with some considerable relief that they caught up with everyone else a few miles further up the road where it got to I-10, on the outskirts of Palm Springs. There Dale swapped bikes back with Tim and then they took a careful look at everyone's bikes to make sure they were all OK.

"Those four wheelers are not getting through that mess," stated Tim.

"Not likely," said Dale.

"No bloody way are they getting after us now!" agreed PJ, looking back up the road just to make sure!

"Damn that was hard work," said Marie, "I hope we don't have to go through anything else like that."

"No guarantees," replied Andy, "But when you think about it we had a real spot of luck, having to get through the fault back there!"

"Yeah," said Tim, "Those bastards would have caught us without that."

"When we get somewhere safe and a long way from here,"

said Kacie, "I'm going to make us all a nice cup of tea!"

"I really need a shot of something stronger," said Dale, then with a smile, "but tea will do just fine!"

Palm Springs and the area around it looked like it had been hit by a tornado, with flattened buildings and swathes of debris everywhere. There was lots of fire damage too.

"Whoo what a mess," said Kacie. "Sure glad I wasn't here when that quake hit."

"Yeah, well they knew the big one was coming," said PJ. "They just figured not in their lifetime. Wonder how many of them managed to claim on their earthquake insurance?"

"You probably can't get quake insurance if you live on a fault line as big as this one," said Kacie.

"Or the premiums are so high it's not worth it," added Heather.

The friends followed I-10 east until they got to Highway 86. This would take them south to the city of El Centro, which was right on the border with Mexico. 86 looked a bit strange, there were no wrecks on it. Kind of eerie this close to a superslab. Then a couple of miles down the road they saw the reason why... more earthquake damage turning the road into a real mess, but it looked like you could get a bike and maybe a four-by-four through on the edge of the road, so PJ dropped down two gears but he had a strange feeling as he did this so he put on a show of going slow, then as he reached a critical point just before the rubble, he gassed it and put all his effort into going as fast as he knew how. It was all pretty much a reflex action based on "selling the dummy" one of his favorite passing techniques when racing.

As he aimed his bike across the edge of the mass of rubble an animal of a man leapt out of his hiding place in the centre of the mess of tarseal and concrete in the middle of the road scaring the hell out of PJ! He was carrying what looked like a sword in one hand and a sawn-off shotgun in the other. He was draped in dirt-grey rags and what looked like a torn-up piece of carpet with a hole for his head. Topping off the carpet he had a bushy beard, dirty long flowing hair, and a *violin* strapped to his back! The man launched himself at PJ yelling like this was a good place to stop and pay a toll, but he misjudged the speed of the bike and PJ got safely past and out of reach. The madman didn't turn fast enough to avoid being side-swiped by Jeff and he was knocked over. As the others rode by, PJ and Jeff covered him with their bows while still astride their bikes. Then they followed everyone else off down the edge of the Salton Sea.

Some twenty miles after they had got by the madman they had a real stroke of luck. There was an abandoned dually pickup with a huge gas tank that was almost full. 86 was a kind of nothing desert road that ran along the western edge of a big lake called the Salton Sea. The road didn't really go anywhere if you needed to escape LA, so that and the earthquake damage was probably why the gas was still there in the pickup.

It was really hot and humid since they had come down out of the mountains and the high desert plains.

"This area is known as being really hot in summer," explained Susan. "But it used to be real pleasant in winter. No way to tell what it will be like in winter now. The Salton Sea used to be a resort place for LA back in the 50's. The resorts and other small places on the shore are ghost towns now."

"How did that happen?" asked Tim.

“The lake is a weird part of nature that has existed on and off over several hundred thousand years. Most recently it was created by a land developer around 1890 who cut a couple of canals from the Colorado river to irrigate the land. Instead he succeeded in flooding the whole area and creating the current lake, which is below sea level incidentally.”

“A *land* developer!” exclaimed Kacie.

Susan continued. “But the lake became more salty than the sea because it’s so hot here and there’s only a few inches of annual rainfall. The rising salt level killed off most of the fish people tried to stock it with. It’s all compounded by fertiliser run off from the farming which creates algae that depletes the oxygen in the water. The main source of water for the lake now is a toxic river that carries sewage and industrial pollutants from Mexico. Bottom line; the lake is a really unhealthy place to be around, lots of pollutants and a shoreline populated with dead birds, dead fish and their skeletons.”

“Don’t reckon I’ll walk over for a dip then!” drawled Tim.

The road alongside the Salton Sea

The girls set up a food break while the guys siphoned the gas out of the pickup until everything they had was full. Just then they heard a strange noise from back the way they had come. As it got louder it sounded like the rather frenetic put-putting of an old gas-powered irrigation pump that had been sitting in the sun too long and had gone a bit, cranky. Then out of the distance on the road appeared a haze of oil smoke in the centre of which was an old "monkey bike", its tiny little tyres whirring away flat out as it approached them at the pace of a high-speed lawn mower. In charge, or more correctly, out of charge of the thing was the crouched figure of the madman, perched on top of what looked like a sack of potatoes on the seat. He had an old leather flying helmet on his head with the straps flapping around behind him and World War One flying goggles. Strapped to his back were his sword, the sawn-off shotgun, and the violin! The monkey bike and rider, surrounded by the haze of oil smoke, slowly, oh so slowly, got bigger as it got closer. It was like watching an animated cartoon in extra slow motion!

The friends just stood there, eyes wide open, as the apparition closed in on them—frozen in whatever they were doing: a mug of coffee halfway to their face or half a sandwich of food partially bitten off in their mouth. Finally the madman pulled up in front of them, sat up and grinned a big toothy smile across the whole of his bearded weather-beaten face.

"Hi y'awl. Sorry about the toll thing, my bad. Figured you were goin' someplace an' maybe I oughter come along. There's no more traffic down this road no-how any-how," he paused and looked at Dale and his eyes opened wide. "Hey—dude, is that coffee?"

The madman parked his machine and accepted a sandwich and a mug of coffee. "Man, you have no idea how good this is," he said as he swallowed nearly half the sandwich in one gulp followed by a big mouthful of coffee. "Mah name's Pete. Ah'm from Texas!"

He removed the flying goggles and, with carefully structured emphasis, replaced them with a set of those awful sunglasses with the fancy upswept ends that American women were wearing back in the 1950s. There was another awestruck pause!

"You can't be too careful when it comes to your eyes!" drawled Tim putting his hand over his mouth and barely containing his laughter. Pete was obviously very satisfied with the response from everyone as he concealed the slight smile on his face with a long slow draught of coffee!

They introduced themselves. Pete had massive hands, huge, and real powerful, but he was careful not to squeeze too hard when he shook hands with anyone. He had a disarmingly childlike manner which appealed to the girls although the guys remained justifiably wary. The girls had huge grins on their faces, and some of the guys too. But if you looked closely, you would have seen Pete was not as crazy as he made out, and was carefully watching their reaction to him under partially hooded eyelids and his big bushy eyebrows, just in case he was in trouble.

PJ looked closely at the monkey bike. "Is this a Tote Gote? It's a Tote Gote! I've only ever seen one before in magazines back in the late 60s."

Pete and the Tote Gote

"Yep," said Pete, "my Daddy bought it new way back before

all them Japanese bikes came on the market. Reliable as all get out. Not very fast though. But that don't make no never no mind nowadays... right?"

"Right!" agreed PJ, "how fast is it, I mean we're going slow but..."

Pete's eyes lit up and he smiled, he was in! "Oh she'll do 30 miles an hour, all day!" But Pete had a look on his face that pretty much betrayed the fact that he had the fingers of both hands crossed behind his back as he said that.

"30? More like 3!" said Dale. "I remember those things, no suspension, no handling, uncomfortable as hell!"

"Well this one's been modified. She'll do at least 15 on the black top."

"Hmm, well I guess you'll keep up if we take it real easy, we've got some bad roads ahead in Baja," said PJ. "But then the Tote Gote was made for the dirt."

Dale was looking at the sack on the seat of the Tote Gote: "You got potatoes in that sack?"

"Yup," answered Pete, "you guys like potatoes?"

PJ's eyes were gleaming. "Man we can sure use those, for seed!"

"Sounds good to me," said Pete. "You guys haven't got any 'all' have you? The old girls running a bit low."

"All? Oh *oil!* You bet," replied Jeff.

So they topped up the 'all' in the crankcase of the little four-stroke Briggs and Stratton engine in the frame under the seat, and filled up the spare gas cans Pete had strapped to the bike.

"Where'd you get the flying helmet from?" asked Tim.

"My great-granddaddy was in the flying corps in World War One. Keeps your head real warm when you sleep. Gets pretty cold at night out in the open."

Everyone lightened the bag of potatoes by fitting as many as they could in the pockets of their clothes; they really didn't want to lose any. Then Pete placed the bag behind him so his weight wouldn't crush the potatoes and put his pack on the seat instead.

"I didn't have time to get sorted out. Figured I needed to get right on after you. The pack is going to be more comfortable to sit on anyhoo!"

"This is probably it for gas," said PJ. "I doubt there'll be anything in Mexico. Hell, half the gas stations didn't have gas back when I visited *before* everything blew up. They sure as hell won't now! I reckon this will get us most of the way down Baja on the east coast and maybe all the way to the west if we're lucky." The west coast was where a lot of the vegetables and such were grown for export to the US and Canada.

"Why are we going down the east coast?" asked Mike.

"When things went bad, the area around San Diego and Tijuana was pretty much a war zone," replied Susan.

"Yeah," added Tim, "there was always a problem with illegal immigration and drug trafficking on our side and the drug lords and the army on their side. Everyone wanted their cut."

Susan continued. "It was a war. The armies of the drug lords and the Mexican Army and Police all fighting each other and joining in... well, everyone else. Our border guards, our police and army and our private militias and gun owners. The whole area exploded or imploded. Whatever," she paused. "We don't want to go there because the chances are we won't get through even now. You can bet there are still some survivors and they'll be the bad guys, the ones with the guns."

“One more long hot summer without enough food will fix all that!” said PJ. “There won’t be anyone left alive.”

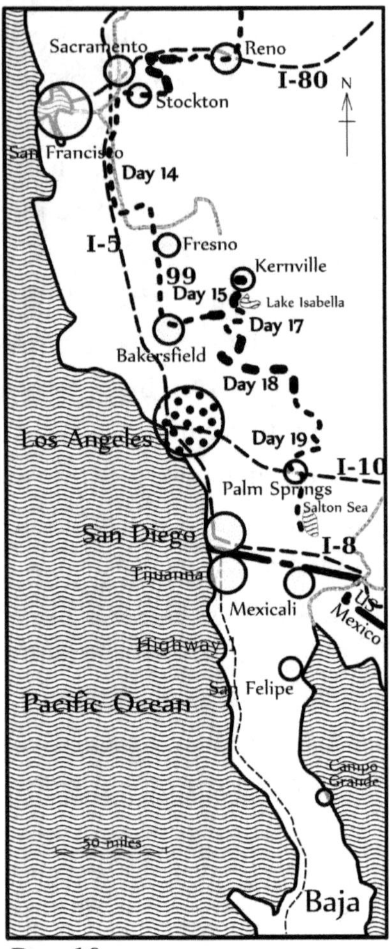

Day 19

It was starting to get dark, so they camped at the southern end of the Salton Sea near some palm trees and found a bunch of pineapples growing in a plantation. The juicy fresh pineapples were the perfect end to a long hot day.

Chapter 14, Baja.

The next morning, the long trail of motorbikes had Pete proudly bringing up the rear with the Tote Gote. They rode through a bunch of wrecks in El Centro without any trouble and crossed the border at Mexicali. Eventually they found their way through the maze of torn up streets from road works in downtown Mexicali and the other streets that were filled with rubbish and abandoned vehicles.

"Man this place is a mess!" said Tim.

"Yeah it hasn't changed one bit since I visited way back," added PJ. "They had the main road all tore up then. Took me hours to find my way out! I had to ask a local. He didn't speak any English nor me Spanish, and all the signs on the roads were in Spanish. We were stuck in a traffic jam on a detour route. He got me sorted out though. Turns out I was heading completely the wrong direction. He was a good guy."

It was easier getting out of town now. PJ had a map of the city. "I had this map back back then as well. But I was so annoyed with the condition of the streets and having to take detours that had no signs, or signs I couldn't read, I forgot all about the map." The girls looked knowingly at each other but were smart enough not to say anything while the guys just grinned!

They headed off down the east coast of Baja on a good tarseal road that crossed a totally barren and inhospitable desert. Sometime later they were in another stretch of empty desert where there was a military checkpoint. A machine gun bunker dug into the middle of the road, covered in camouflage netting. It had a diversion off the tarseal onto the side of the road to slow you down. It was abandoned now, but still real scary to approach because you couldn't see if anyone was under the netting. Just a single machine gun would wipe them all out in a few seconds.

The desert road south of Mexicali

Pete was getting the Tote Gote up close to 20 mph on the flat and every eight or ten miles or so everyone else would stop and wave him by until he more or less disappeared into the distance. Then they would start back up and overtake him until they had gone another eight or ten miles. Each time Pete passed them he would put his head down and make believe twist the throttle wide open even more. He would grasp the left fork downtube with his left hand like a flat-tracker and make like he was racing them and everyone would cheer!

The bad road on the east coast of Baja

About 50 miles south of San Felipe this good road changed into one of the worst dirt roads any of them had ever been on. They were truly in the wilds now, climbing up and down the hills near the ocean. There was no sign of civilization apart from the road and almost no vegetation, just dry grass and absolutely nothing green. It was really tough going and they were down to first gear in many places, struggling for their balance where the road had eroded down to bedrock. While these places slowed the bigger bikes like crazy, Pete and the Tote Gote just kept on truckin'. At these bad places Dale and Heather stopped and let Evie and Will walk, this was good for the kids to stretch their legs and made it much easier for the two of them to ride the bikes.

One of the valleys where the road had washed away

There was a ferocious strong wind following them; sweeping unchecked across the treeless open hills and valleys, and they were all covered in a fine white powdery dust. In a few places in the valleys near the ocean the road had been completely washed away, so they fought the bikes through the loose sandy dirt and silt. This was especially tough for the lesser skilled riders. They fell off a lot and there were many stops to help them pick up their bikes and push them to get going again. Before they descended into these places PJ would make careful note of where the road was on the other side of the valley. That way he could guide everyone in the right direction on the shortest route once they got to the bottom and the road had disappeared.

It took them all day but finally they reached an abandoned gas station and turned left off the main road. There they arrived at an idyllic place on the ocean called Campo Grande. There were the remains of a string of beach cottages plus a small hotel and restaurant and even a small airstrip.

PJ looked at the wreckage of the restaurant. "I had some good meals here. There was a guy and his wife on a Paris-Dakar bike holed up at the hotel. They had relied on getting gas at the gas station out by the main dirt road. It was empty and everyone was waiting for the gas tanker to get here. When I arrived they'd been here for a week with the tanker coming everyday: 'tomorrow'. Manyana, I guess. The young couple didn't seem to mind. Well... good food, lovely weather, great beach, nothing to do except sit in the bar with a cool one. Bummer!"

"You had enough gas?" asked Dale.

PJ grinned. "You bet, I've driven across the Sahara. I know what it's like in these places!"

It looked like a huge tidal surge or wave had swept through these parts, wiping out most of the strip of buildings on the thin sand bar next to the sea. There was the tail section of a light plane sticking up out of some sand dunes inland. There were lots of erosion gullies with sheets of plywood, timber, and corrugated iron and other pieces of buildings. And there were a few vehicles scattered and half-buried all over the place. Amongst all this human detritus there were scrubby bushes still growing in the sandy ground. Strangely enough, there was a small dinghy tied up and floating at the water's edge. Another survivor, just like them.

"When I drove through here a few years ago," said PJ. "I was up high out on a desolate stretch of this road near the sea, taking photos, when a good-looking lady in a Subaru stopped to say hi and see if I was OK. She had one hand on the steering wheel and the other holding a bottle of Mexican beer! I was a bit worried about getting through in my two-wheel drive, but she said if I'd made it that far I wouldn't have any trouble, but that if I did break down or whatever to find someone with a phone and she would help. Just ask for the Plywood Princess, she said. Everyone knows me! Struck me then that if you could live in a region so barren and rough and unpopulated, and drive down a road that bad chugging on a beer, that this might well be a very good place to live! I wonder what happened to her?"

"From the look of this mess I'd guess everyone on the coastline bought it," said Jeff.

"Oh well..." said PJ.

The pelicans fishing

Here on the beach they bathed and cleaned up in the ocean, and just behind them at a lagoon watched a flock of pelicans swooping and diving into the shallow waters after fish. The wind slowed to a gentle breeze and all the pounding and hardship of the journey seeped slowly away as they floated in the warm water or lay down and rested on the sandy shore.

Behind them the sun went down over the lagoon and the sands on the golden beach turned shades of black for the night. They went to sleep in the pleasant light cool breeze coming off the ocean, lulled by the tiny night waves swishing on the sand.

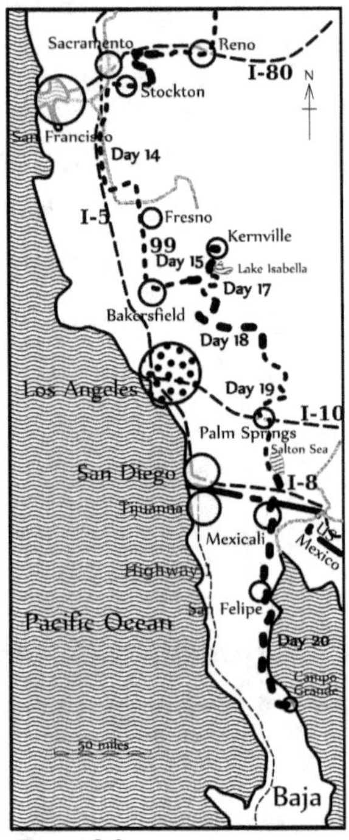

Day 20

The next day they woke to the sunrise coming over the ocean, more peaceful it seemed, than any they had ever seen. Then came the breeze over the land, making patterns on the smooth water, and sweeping these patterns with them heading out to sea. Beneath the glistening surface the mornings slowly waking ocean sent baby wavelets to make small "get out of bed" sounds on the beach.

Swish. "Wake up, your morning is here, your day is ready."
Swish. "Wake up."
Swish. "Wake up."
Swish.
It was so easy to lie back and forget all about the road.

Sunrise at Campo Grande

The wind picked up, until it was blowing hard as they made ready to leave. A flock of white cranes floated into the lagoon, cruising almost motionless above the water as they headed into the strong wind. They landed on a tide bar to join a group of black pelicans standing in the breaking waters of the shallows. There they stood, small pillars of white and black, motionless against the now turbulent sea.

They set off again on the bad dirt road, knowing that they would reach the main highway near the west coast around mid-day if all went well. Now they were getting into huge stands of cactus all around them, especially in the valleys. In many places on either side of the official roadway there were sandy tracks that were way smoother than the road. But these required constant attention to keeping their balance to avoid sliding off the bikes in the places where the sand was deep.

The road itself was awful as it had a surface of embedded small rocks, so if you chose the road it was like riding on a jack hammer. Everything shook and things vibrated loose and fell off and your hands became numb. This was one of the roads used by the famous Baja 1000 race.

Embedded small rocks on the bad road heading west from Campo Grande

If you took to the tracks on the side it was much smoother but you had to be a real good rider to avoid coming off and taking a tumble in the sand. So the better riders had fun going fast in the sand while the others went real slow either in the sand or on the bumpy main track. Actually in sand, it's better if you do go fast—there's very little traction in sand, but by going fast you spread out the traction you need over a greater distance. It's a dynamic technique that takes skill and confidence. If you don't have this technique and instead you go slow it means you tumble off the bike just the same as if you went fast, only slower!

They had to stop often to allow the slower ones, and Pete of course, to catch up and then wait while they had a break as well. Plus they had to fix the things on the bikes that were coming loose all the time with the extreme vibration from the road. One thing that kept them going though, was that they were almost there, almost at their goal!

Cactus on the side of the road

"It's very beautiful around here, just like a nature reserve," said Kacie looking all around on one of their stops.

"Everything on the whole continent is going to be a nature reserve now," added Jeff. "That'll keep the greenies happy, if any of them are still alive."

The main highway down through Baja

The main highway was tarseal and it was such a treat after all they had been through. It was plain sailing with no wrecks or mess and they made good time heading north until they came out at what had once been a little village. It had fruit trees and cultivated fields in a small valley near the coast. The village had been damaged by looting and fire and was deserted now. So here they stopped and parked the bikes for good. Next spring they would have to make the journey north on foot.

That evening they sat very quietly together around a small fire, there was no more rush and uncertainty about tomorrow. It was time for them to get started on settling in.

"I guess this is our winter land now," said PJ.

"This will do just fine," said Kacie.

Mike looked at the fire and smiled. "Y'know, for the longest time I never thought we would make it, but by golly we're a bunch of survivors!"

Heather clapped her hands. "Well done everyone!"

"Yes," said Marie. "I feel like we should take the day off tomorrow!"

"Well we don't have to rush any more," Tim said.

"Yep," agreed Pete. "Ahm definitely feeling like a day off from riding the Tote Gote, I've got me a very sore bum!"

"None of us can get away from 'monkey-butt' when we're riding a bike all day!" added Kacie.

PJ looked around the group encircling the fire. "It's good for us to take a break. Tim's right, there's no rush as long as we get the seeds in the ground. Time has slowed down for us, the years will go much slower now; but the day is the same so we will live through the same number of sunrises and sunsets." He paused. "We'll still live the same number of days; we just won't know how old we are when we die." He paused again. "But then when we do get old we will still be ready to die."

There was silence all around, with just the fire crackling and making small snuffling noises as everyone looked deep into the flames. Evie broke the spell. "Are we all going to have gardens?"

"Too right!" answered PJ. "Would you like one each or one big one between the two of you?"

"I want one big one!" said Will.

"I don't mind," said Evie.

"Well, you can have one big one. But we may have to split it up a bit and give you several smaller plots," PJ paused while he thought about it. "Actually we should all do that, it's easier to look after smaller plots when you're doing everything by hand," he smiled and looked around at the faces lit up by the fire. "First thing we have to do though is till the land and get the seeds planted."

"Y'know," said Kacie, "we don't have to take an actual break. We've been three weeks on the road, scared out of our minds at times, being chased and shot at. Spending pretty much every day not knowing what will come at us next. Figuring out where we're going to plant all the crops, then tilling the land and planting the seeds... that will be just the break we need!"

It was very peaceful as they watched the flames flickering away and the ashes making small crunching noises as the firewood settled. Their travels were over for now, but overhead, the Milky Way reminded them that their journey would come again as the stars travelled slowly and silently across the sky on their constant journey through the night.

There is no way to know the future of course, but with that magical roof of twinkling stars overhead, it was hard not to have a pretty good feeling about life.

Kacie had a strong baby boy. Wendy asked Kacie what giving birth was like and Kacie replied that it was *really really* bad.

"As bad as having a bad crash on a Trials bike?" asked PJ.

"Way worse, you guys have no idea!"

"I've had two crash-damaged legs coming off a Trials bike where I couldn't walk and a lot of pain," said PJ, "took me over a week to recover enough that I could get around. Trying to sleep when there's no position where it doesn't hurt. Deciding if I really wanted to go to the can upstairs... maybe I could hold on. Those are bad times when you live alone."

"Trust me PJ, having a baby is worse!"

Dale and Sandy were hanging out together and the Boneman was happily shacked up with Susan. PJ was fiercely independent. He had been married once and had had enough of all that nonsense! He had no problems living alone and was quite happy spending all his time in his beloved garden. Andy and June were doing just fine as were Jason and Sam, and Tim and Marie were happily living together; but Wendy? Ahh now Wendy seemed to

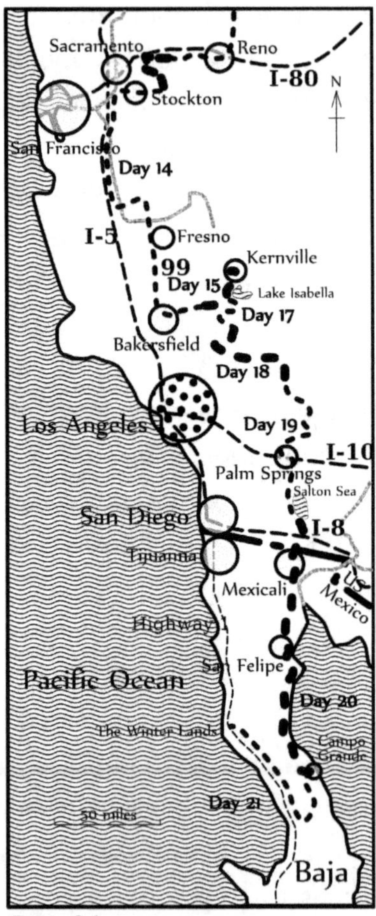

Day 21

be spending quite a bit of time asking all kinds of advice from

PJ to help her with her garden! The California kids Evie and Will were adopted by Pete and everybody except Alex and Pete were pretty much paired off in their tight little community even Jeff with Heather. She was a fine lady and the two of them got along real well. They both liked to keep to themselves though so they set up in separate places, but not too far away from each other.

Everyone learned how to plant and grow food from PJ, except that PJ kept away from Marie. "She can figure it out from someone else, I don't need to get my face punched again!"

At the end of winter when it was time to harvest, they had a small celebration and a feast where they all told their favourite stories from long ago, from way back in the days when all you had to do was press a button for entertainment. Pete played his violin, rather well actually; he had obviously had some classical training. Tim, Dale, and the Boneman did a "Barber Shop" routine where everyone joined in the chorus. PJ was persuaded to tell some of his African stories and he told the one about how he nearly got killed by a Panga gang that attacked him late at night while he slept, and he escaped in his underpants on his Yamaha Trials bike.

"What's a Panga?" asked Will.

"Do you know what a Machete is?" Will nodded. "It's the same thing."

Evenings, when they sat overlooking the beach and the setting sun, and watched the Pacific Ocean rollers coming in, it looked like they and everyone with them were going to make it—and make it perhaps into a better future after all.

End of Part 1.

The author.

Bill (Billy d) de Garis was born in England, grew up in New Zealand and spent several years travelling around the world. First on a 250cc Jawa motorbike from Sydney, Australia through India, Afghanistan and Iran to England; then an epic journey in an old Morris Isis shooting-brake (running mostly on bald tyres salvaged from rubbish dumps around London) together with two New Zealand friends on their honeymoon. The journey started in London, went across the Sahara desert and darkest Africa and ended up in Kenya. He now lives in Port Moody, a city-suburb of Vancouver in British Columbia, Canada. He has been writing short stories and poetry since the late 1960s. He is better known as an off-road motorcycle competitor in East Africa (seven times Kenya motorcycle champion) but also raced on tarseal—in India and Sri Lanka he won several roadraces including the Air India Grand Prix in Bombay (now Mumbai). He is also the first person to climb Mt. Kilimanjaro (19,340ft) on a motorbike (250cc CZ). He now competes on a Gas Gas Trials motorbike in the US National Trials Championship.

This is his first novel.

His second novel (published Dec 2014) is **2020 The Long Walk**

The third novel (published October 2016) is **2020 Africa**

www.ingramcontent.com/pod-product-compliance
Lightning Source LLC
LaVergne TN
LVHW020714110826
845149LV00012B/2263